THE COURT JESTERS

THE COURT JESTERS

a novel by AVIGDOR DAGAN

translated by Barbara Harshav

THE JEWISH PUBLICATION SOCIETY
Philadelphia · New York   5749 / 1989

Copyright © 1989 by Avigdor Dagan
First edition   All rights reserved
Manufactured in the United States of America
Library of Congress Cataloging in Publication Data

Dagan, Avigdor 1912:
    [Letsane he-hatser. English]
    The court jesters: a novel / Avigdor Dagan; translated by
Barbara Harshav.—1st ed.
        p.   cm.
    Translation of: Letsane he-hatser.
    ISBN 0-8276-0324-X
    1. Holocaust, Jewish (1939-1945)—Fiction.   I. Title.
PJ5054. D2195L4813   1989
892.4'36—dc19   89-1659
                                                               CIP

Designed by Adrianne Onderdonk Dudden

THE COURT JESTERS

** 1*

Believe me, I really don't want to talk about myself. But how can you follow my story if you don't know anything about the narrator? All I can do is ask you to be patient.

Everybody here calls me "The Judge," even though it's been a long time since I presided over a courtroom. In fact, I never was a judge here in Israel. Long before I came to Jerusalem, I decided to hang up my judge's robe once and for all and never wrap myself in it again.

Why? Well, here's where my troubles start. How do you make the crooked straight? I really don't want to have to go back to Adam, but what can I do? What I have to tell happened on the day I was born.

My father, a young judge in those days—and in this

respect, as in others, I followed in his footsteps—had been transferred to a court in another district just about the time I was due to make my entry into this world. As my mother's labor pains began, the devil decided to brew up a storm that night the likes of which no one had ever seen before in his life. It broke branches, uprooted trees, tore up roots, and swept a tangle of electrical poles and wires down the streets.

Maybe that storm hastened my birth. I was born by the light of hastily found candles and kerosene lamps whose empty bellies first had to be filled. The maid, called to hold the lamp, dropped it when a lightning bolt split an old lime tree in the yard. Under such strange circumstances was I welcomed into the world.

Then the midwife gave the newborn infant to a nurse to hold before he was washed. As the lightning struck, the nurse shrieked horribly, seeing a pillow on my mother's bed catch fire. The flames quickly spread through the room. In a fraction of a second, before she recovered from the shock, I slipped out of her hands and dropped onto the hard floor.

I'm told that I didn't cry. Maybe even then I learned to roll with the punches and keep my mouth shut. The doctor, who was summoned even before they put out the fire, only shrugged and said we had to wait to be completely sure the fall didn't have any consequences but he didn't find any evidence of serious damage. Strange as it may seem, he added, he was sure that children had their own guardian angels.

Evidently, however, the guardian angel assigned to me wasn't paying much attention to his duties just then for, soon enough, when they tried to teach me to stand up and walk, it became clear that something wasn't quite right with my spine. As I grew bigger, the hump on my back grew more prominent and my head sank deeper and deeper between my fragile shoulders.

Later on in school, when I easily caught up with and overtook my classmates in most subjects, they told me I had been given an especially quick brain to make up for that blow. Afterward, when the others went to dancing lessons and went walking in the evening along the old city walls or under the lime trees in bloom along the river, when you could find couples hugging at every step, I would gladly have traded all the cleverness in the world for one touch of a girl's lips. I got over that too. I reconciled myself to everything, even the hump sitting on my back that never leaves me for a moment.

Soon I began to believe that in my hump I carried a secret key to open gates for me that are locked to others, so that I can see what is invisible to everybody else and can guess what they can't.

These were all qualities I once attributed to my father. I loved and admired him more than anybody else in the world. To me he was omnipotent. I believed, for example, that he had wings. Not like the angels, since he didn't even have to stretch out his arms. It was only in his dreams that he had the power to fly. He could hover over the roofs of the city, peep into windows, light on a windowsill, and sing a lullaby to a weeping child. Yes, I believed that, even when he was sitting on his judge's bench, his mind soared off far away from the court and landed in the place where the crime was committed; he flew backward in time—for he could do that too—to see how and why events happened as they did and then could return in time to pass judgment without paying too much attention to what was said during the trial.

I wasn't the only one who believed that. The whole city whispered such things. That was the only way people could explain the fact that none of my father's rulings was ever overruled by higher courts. In fact, it was enough to come to our house on a Sunday afternoon and see him sitting in his rocking chair next to the window, looking at the crown of the old chestnut tree in front of the house. He would sit like that for hours and hours, an open book in his lap, without giving any sign that he sensed what was going on behind his back in that very room. Anyone who saw him like that even once could have no doubt that he was hovering somewhere far away at that very moment.

Then I began to sense the same quality in myself. Maybe I inherited it from my father, but I still believed that it had something to do with the heavy burden stuck on my back, which had no rhyme or reason unless it also concealed some invisible blessing.

After my father's death I took to sitting not only on his chair next to the window, but also on the judge's bench where he had sat for so long. Now it was my turn. Though I knew all the documents and the testimony, my mind hovered over the city and over distant places till it sensed the truth. But I didn't have the force of Father's personality. I lacked his courage to decide on the strength of my intuition rather than on the dead letter of the files. In many trials, I was convinced that things didn't happen as the evidence seemed to indicate. For I had seen the truth with my own eyes. But how could I prove that the truth I knew in my dreams—what else could I call this special experience that was surely like my father's?—was really the truth? How can a man pass judgment when the proof in his hands doesn't come from the same world as the evidence he has to accept as a judge?

How often did I wish that, unlike my father's, the higher court would overturn some decision of mine. Because in my verdicts, based on the law and nothing but the law, there wasn't the slightest grain of the truth as I knew it. If I had confessed, if I had given the smallest hint of how I arrived at the truth, they would have thrown me off the judge's bench immediately. A few hundred years ago, even not so long as that, I would have ended up burned at the stake. In my day, maybe behind the high walls of a mental institution. And I was afraid of that, for I didn't inherit Father's courage. That's why I couldn't go on being a judge. But my actual decision came in the wake of events of a very different order.

Later, in the hell of the camp ruled by the almighty Major Kohl, I witnessed thousands of things that reinforced my doubts about whether any man has the right to judge his fellow man. Kohl, lord of life and death in that place—and all of us were half dead anyway—didn't need a stake or a mental institution either. He didn't even need to waste a bullet to get rid of me if he felt like it. All he had to do was throw me out into the freezing night or set the dogs on me or send me to one of the mad criminals who called themselves doctors and were eager to get their hands on a hunchback for their satanic experiments.

Fortunately for me, Major Kohl wasn't at all interested in how I knew and saw things that were invisible to everyone else. Only one thing was important to him: how to exploit this ability of mine for his own profit. But even before word of what was called my sharpsightedness reached Kohl—and I still don't know how—I had gone through enough to know that, if I managed to get out of that hell alive, I could never be a judge again.

We were all starving to death. I knew petty thieves who turned into murderers to satisfy their hunger for a moment with a moldy piece of bread they had stolen from another prisoner. Did I have the right to judge them? I knew a German guard who used to bring us food and saved some of our lives while endangering his own. And I saw the same man, at a slight nod from the sergeant who led our group to work in the quarry, not hesitate for a moment to use his rifle butt to split open the head of a man who fell out of line while marching. Did I have the right to judge him?

When I got to Jerusalem, I didn't tell anyone about my past on the judge's bench. If I grew wise at all in those difficult years, it was the wisdom of the humble: I learned the importance of being unimportant. Yet on my street that leads to Jaffa Gate, there are no secrets. Somehow—in spite of all my precautions—the rumor spread that I used to wear the judge's robes and so now everyone calls me "Judge." And sometimes a foreman comes to me with two apprentices who got into a fight, or they come to me themselves and want me to decide who's right and who's wrong. I don't look for excuses and I don't refuse to listen to both sides, but in the end I tell them something that sounds more like good advice than a judgment and they usually accept what I say.

Now, when age adds its weight to the burden on my back, I've come to terms with my lot and I have nothing to worry about. Every now and then, I collect a few pennies from the neighbors who ask me to write some petition or report for them or sometimes just a letter to a relative overseas. Sometimes I walk along Queen Shlomzion Street until it runs into Jaffa Road and turn right at the Russian Compound. Opposite the church, in a few old buildings, are the offices of the lower courts, and from time to time I can help someone there who can't afford a lawyer's fees. But that's really all that's left of my legal past and I don't remember it even in my dreams.

What I do remember, what I can never forget, what I still dream about—those are quite different things.

*
*
2

Two dreams keep coming back to me more often than any other's. In the first, I'm in a tightly packed cattlecar. People are dying all around me on the long trip with no food, no water, no air.

My neighbor and I are half standing, half lying, leaning against one another, and all of a sudden, he asks me: "You know what sign you were born under?"

"Gemini," I answer.

"Good," he says. "Like me. We'll get through this together."

Then, while thousands around us die ghastly deaths, Max Himmelfarb, my neighbor in the cattlecar, and I, just the two of us, are selected to serve in the court of the almighty Major Kohl, commandant of the death camp where we've been sent.

Court jesters, that's what we're to be. Kohl already had two others: a Jewish dwarf called Leo Riesenberg, an ironic name that makes you think of a lion stretched on high mountains. The other one was the juggler Adam Wahn, whose talent and agility never ceased to amaze and charm our almighty lord and protector.

We never found out why, of all the people in the camp, he decided to put the two of us in his private circus. We could only guess that maybe some officer in our previous camp told him that Max Himmelfarb could read the stars and rumor had it that the hunchback was endowed with the ability to predict the future, see things far away and sometimes even know things that were going to happen in a day or two.

If Max really knew it from the stars, then the stars were right about the two of us surviving. While others were sent to death, Kohl protected his four court jesters like costly curios in a precious collection. The dwarf did handstands, Max read the stars, the juggler taught the major all sorts of card tricks, and my advantage for our lord was that, from time to time, I could guess when the next surprise inspection would take place and I was never wrong. This warning was evidently very important to the commandant, for Kohl was never stingy in his appreciation.

But that's the second dream that keeps coming back to me, more often than any other.

3

We must have been a pretty sight. The striped tatters we wore, like all the other thousands of prisoners, hung on us as on scarecrows. There was a big room—you could almost call it a hall—where Kohl, our almighty lord of life and death, entertained his guests. Every time the door opened, we would run in like circus clowns bursting into the ring, but also like slaves in the Coliseum thrown to the mercy of the wild beasts, for we were never sure we'd get out of there alive.

Kohl had two dogs, a German Shepherd named Wolf and a Great Dane called Brutus. They would start to bark at us as soon as we came in, and there was always a short pause until they could be calmed down and returned, growling, to

13

lie under the long table in the middle of the room and we could start running around in circles.

Most of the time I ran in front of the others, waving my arms and imitating a bird but, because of my hump and my head deep down in my shoulders, looking more like a bat. Behind me, with long hopping steps as if he were in a hurry, came Max Himmelfarb, the tallest one, holding a cardboard cylinder, the kind you use to wrap pictures, raising it over and over again to his innocent, pale blue eyes and pretending he was peering at the stars. Then came the juggler Wahn, throwing bottles high into the air, letting them spin in their orbit and catching them one by one, only to throw them back up and spin them once again.

Leo Riesenberg came last, the dwarf who always had the greatest success with the guests, especially the women. He would toddle in on his short little legs, rolling his head, slipping around between the guests' feet, amazing everyone with his bold somersaults. He would climb up on the table and stand on his head and, when the astonished guests held their breath, he would suddenly ask something like: "Gentlemen, why are you all standing on your head?"

Or he would clamber up on the juggler's shoulders, catch the bottles Wahn had tossed up, put them in a basket one by one, and again ask a startling question: "Why are all the people in this market so small?"

Our performance was, in fact, always the same, even if Adam Wahn sometimes changed his bottles for plates or colored billiard balls. But the dwarf's inventiveness seemed to be infinite. He never told the same joke twice and his jokes never failed to produce waves of laughter. The guests would applaud and the Major would always give him a reward. Sometimes he'd throw him an apple or a piece of cheese or some other delicacy. Then all four of us would crawl under the table and, while the two dogs slept, we'd divide the loot like brothers.

Half a life separates me from the years I spent as one of almighty Major Kohl's court jesters, but I still dream about that more than about anything else. Over and over, all around us, people just like us are dying by the thousands. We four court jesters, we're the only ones who survive everything and everyone.

Every single time I wake up from that dream, I always ask: Why? Why just the four of us? Every single time I wake up to a new day, I tell myself all over again that it's childish to expect an answer. And yet I can't stop asking.

4

Whenever Kohl invited only a few senior officers to a light supper and a glass of wine after a business meeting, the burden would fall mainly on Max Himmelfarb and me. With larger groups, including women, we usually played second fiddle and the juggler and the dwarf bore the brunt. Even when there were only a few guests, Adam Wahn would sometimes take part in the entertainment with a few card tricks from his rich repertoire, and sometimes the dwarf Riesenberg would tell them a couple of jokes. But on such occasions we knew that Kohl was counting on the two of us most of all. I was supposed to tell the guests about dark corners of their past that they themselves couldn't discover. Fortunately, I was allowed to talk with each of them separately. Max was supposed to read their future in the stars.

I don't know which of us had the harder job. I never knew how seriously Max took the stars. He firmly believed that the two of us would survive together because we were born under the sign of Gemini. On the other hand, I don't have a shadow of a doubt that what he revealed to Kohl's guests was nothing but stuff and nonsense, old Gypsy tales, cloaked in more intelligent terms. Yet every now and then he must have hit on some intuition—or the stars were indeed correct—since more than once I heard Kohl singing his praises when some important guest intimated that one of his stargazer's visions had come true. Not only come true but was amazingly precise in several details.

My own case was a bit different. Max could pretend he was reading the stars. But I really did see things, and it wasn't always easy to decide what to hide and what to reveal. It was even harder to make up my mind since what I saw wasn't always limited to the past and didn't even always stay in the present but went a bit further, into the near future.

One day, for instance, I was looking into the past of one of Kohl's guests. A senior officer in love with the beautiful young wife of one of his adjutants. The officer had arranged to have the adjutant sent off to the front while he himself took complete (and not altogether paternal) care of the young beauty—with her willing consent. By then their affair had been going on for a few months. What I saw at that moment was that, unfortunately, the cuckolded husband had just been wounded in Russia. I went as far as I could, and maybe a little bit further than was good for me, and hinted to the lascivious colonel that his mistress's life was in danger. Since my own life was dear to me, I couldn't tell him what else I knew about his future, which was that the adjutant was about to be released from a military hospital and would soon come home on leave without any warning, find his wife in bed with the colonel, kill the two of them on the spot and be killed in battle himself when he returned to the front.

That's only one example of our difficulties. Max and I had a tacit agreement never to say anything in our performances to upset the rulers of our world. For it was absolutely clear to both of us that even the trace of a cloud on the brow of one of Kohl's important guests could be fatal for us. No shadow could fall between any guest and the host who was our lord of life and death. We kept this agreement as carefully as we valued our lives.

Until one night—I have to tell you about what happened that night—when Max broke the rules of the game and went beyond the limit. It was at a party with a lot of guests and though, as always at such occasions, the juggler and the dwarf were supposed to come first, the stargazer and the hunchback seer also had to do their bit. I would tell the men what was in their pockets and reveal to the women the date of their lovers' birthdays while Max strode around the room with long, quick steps that looked like hops, peering through his cardboard telescope and, every now and then, telling what he had just read in the stars.

"This week," he began, "is a good week for Libra and Capricorn. But I see danger for Leo, Taurus, and Scorpio. Those people better not go on long trips this week, certainly not overseas. They'd better not do anything dangerous; they should stay home as much as they can and beware of those they consider friends. I don't see much hope this week for Aries and Cancer either, and I would also advise them to be very very careful."

He thrashed around like that, leaving no straw unbroken, only stopping here and there, pretending to look at the stars through his telescope. Everyone was dazed by him even though—and maybe because—no one was sure how seriously to take his words. Sometimes he sounded like a prophet and sometimes like a mocking chatterbox, like a real court jester who had everything but those little bells that clowns used to wear on their hats and sleeves in real courts centuries ago. Every now and then, he'd tell a couple of jokes, with a casual interjection, like "And as for virgins born under the sign of Virgo, I would urge them strongly to stay virgins for one more week."

The ladies giggled, a bit ashamed, and the men burst out laughing, when Max suddenly turned serious and began to shout something strange that had absolutely nothing to do with what he had just said.

"How can you read the stars?" we heard him shout as he looked out the window again at the dark sky. "How can you read the stars when you can't tell the difference between the stars and the sparks from the ovens burning day and night? When you don't know what's rain and what's blood falling down from heaven?"

For a moment, we were all petrified, stunned with terror at the words that shouldn't have been said.

We all stopped still, breathless—except for little Leo Riesenberg, who was greater than all of us at that moment and needed only a split second to know what he had to do. Nimble as a monkey, he climbed up on the table and jumped over the juggler's shoulder onto the astrologer's neck. Sitting on his shoulders, he rode him, muzzled his mouth with one hand and hit his forehead with the other, all the while shouting like a street peddler singing the praises of his wares.

"Stars, ladies and gentlemen? Stars? They look best when you have bees in your bonnet. Here, one is stinging you. Boom! Now another one. Boom!—And another—Boom!— And another—Boom! You never saw so many stars in front of your eyes. Stars! Stars!"

He went on hitting Max's brow and pinching his face, licking his little fingers over and over and praising the honey made by the imaginary bees in the hive of the astrologer's head. All the time, he sat on Max's long neck, and it looked so funny that the frozen smiles on the faces of Kohl's guests thawed and they all began to laugh out loud and slapped each other on the back.

Max, in the meantime, had recovered his senses, got back into his role, and ran around the long table in the middle of the room with the dwarf riding on his shoulders. Suddenly, it all looked like the carefully rehearsed performance of a couple of clowns. After a while, in full control of himself, the astrologer went back to his horoscopes.

"Those born under the sign of Gemini," he said, "may also find themselves in danger, but God is watching over them."

He knew very well that the almighty Major Kohl had also been born under that sign.

5

Over and over again, it seemed as if a gust of wind suddenly blew through Max Himmelfarb's head, making a mess of the card catalog of his memory where he had noted everything so carefully. It took him a while to make order again and put every card back into the right drawer. But until he did, he would say things that seemed to have no rhyme or reason and that no one understood. Usually all he needed was a little bit of quiet and, except for that one incident where he was saved by Leo Riesenberg's quick thinking, the occasional disturbances in the astrologer's train of thought really didn't concern us very much. Anyway, I knew where it all came from.

In the court of Major Kohl, we had more than enough

time to share our memories with each other. The court jesters of the mighty camp commandant went to work every morning like everybody else, but their overseers had clear instructions not to give them hard tasks, so we came back to camp less exhausted than the others. But since Kohl didn't use us every night, we had ample opportunity to talk. The circumstances of our conversations encouraged confessions we wouldn't have dreamed of making in other times, with other people.

I remember, for instance, what Max told me about his father's death.

Professor Emil Bernhard Himmelfarb, famous mathematician, honorary member of God knows how many scientific societies in various countries, member of the academy, winner of countless prizes and distinctions, lay dying in a large, well-heated room whose tall windows were covered with thick drapes. The whole family was gathered around ... and everyone was listening carefully, holding their breath, waiting anxiously for the few words struggling to get past the dying man's bloodless lips:

"I don't know. Don't know. Don't know."

Max told me he had never heard anything more desperate in his life than these last words with the last breath of his dying father. The famous scientist, the father whose sons had always heard from his admirers that he knew everything, admitted in his last moments that he didn't know. After all the praise and all the success, this was the summing up of the last account, this was the last message he left his sons as a legacy:

"I don't know. Don't know. Don't know."

Even after they closed the dead man's eyes and began to get ready for the funeral, even as he was reading the

Kaddish with his brother over the open grave and didn't understand the words of the prayer, even then Max heard nothing else but:

"I don't know. Don't know. Don't know."

He heard neither the rabbi's eulogy nor the speeches of the rector and the officials of the university. The only thing he heard, over and over again, were those words that burst out of his father's heavy lips as he passed away. Every clump of earth thrown into the grave, falling on his father's coffin, seemed to echo: I don't know. Don't know. Don't know.

"Nothing is engraved deeper in my memory," Max Himmelfarb said when he told me of his father's death. And I couldn't ever forget it either.

I also remember what he told me about his family. His brother Felix was eight years his senior. There had been times when they didn't have much in common because of the difference in age—as when Felix was a young man of twenty and Max a boy of twelve. But later on they would talk until late at night about what was on their minds. Max always felt safe when Felix was nearby, and Felix quickly became more serious than most men his age because he had to take care of his little brother.

Between them, four years older than Max and four years younger than Felix, was a sister both brothers adored. Martha was beautiful, jollier than the two boys, and she played the piano delightfully well. She filled the usually quiet house with carefree song and the laughter of thousands of little bells—the best cure for every sorrow. Just before her eighteenth birthday, their mother died suddenly. From that day on Martha took over the housekeeping chores and filled her mother's place so well that it seemed as if she had never thought of doing anything else.

Three years later, after their father's death, Martha became the real head of the household, and neither Max, still a pupil in the gymnasium, nor Felix, an assistant to the well-known astronomer Professor Hagen, thought for a moment that maybe this was not the proper or the only solution. Of course they pretended to participate in making decisions, but they all knew that, in the end, they would accept what Martha thought was right. Her word, always accompanied by a flash of laughter in her eyes and the prettiest smile on her lips, was a law unto them even before it was spoken. Wherever she was there was sunshine and light. She scolded her brothers only for steeping themselves in books and not enjoying life as they should.

"What about you?" they would retort. "You should have had a husband and children a long time ago. We should be uncles by now."

"Me?" she would smile. "First I have to see the two of you married. Then it'll be my turn."

"So you'll make us marry the first girls we see just to save you from being an old maid."

"Don't worry about me," she would conclude, and a merry laugh would resound in the house. "Better go and enjoy yourselves or you'll crumble like dry leaves."

Then one day, when Felix was already a senior lecturer, "Herr Dozent," and Max was in the last years of his studies, the sun went down. Martha fell ill, the doctors found that she had leukemia, and less than half a year later the brothers were left alone. Once again they came back from the cemetery, and there was silence for a long time until Max—who had always turned to his older brother when he himself had no answer—asked Felix the question.

"Why?"

After a while, he asked again: "Why? Tell me why."

As before with his father, Max believed that Felix knew everything and could find an answer for everything. But Felix could only repeat what they had heard years before from the lips of their dying father: "I don't know. Don't know. Don't know."

Then, as he told me later in Major Kohl's court, Max, who ever since his father's death had made peace with the idea that there would be many things he would never know, now knew that one of the mysteries he would never solve was why Martha, full of life as a meadow full of flowers — why she, of all the people in the world, had to die so young.

And, he told me, he also knew this: that, if there is a God, as they had taught him when he was a child and as he had believed for so many years until Martha's death — if there is a God, he would never be able to love Him again.

6

What else did I know about Max Himmelfarb? Did I know what always made him forget where he was and suddenly made him say things that had nothing to do with what was said before?

I knew that after he got his degree in history he worked in the library of his alma mater. He felt best there, among the books arranged so neatly on the shelves. Everything was in its place and, even if he hadn't read each and every book, he knew what was in all of them and his clockwork memory was famous among the students and his colleagues. He could give them detailed bibliographies on every subject in history as if he pulled it out of his sleeve.

He didn't have great ambitions for himself. Occasionally

he would publish a little piece of research in one of the scientific journals that were published in Germany at that time, but he knew that his work wasn't very original. Like a mole, his forte was patiently digging and exposing everything that was ever written on a given subject and then comparing, arranging, categorizing, and sorting the conclusions that others had reached. He didn't suffer from an excess of self-esteem. What if his work didn't mean much? Maybe, one day, some great historian with broad vision and deep intuition would decide to develop this very same subject. And maybe this great historian would lack that modest little quality with which he, Max Himmelfarb, was so richly endowed.

Sometimes as he worked grotesque thoughts would come into his head. He was capable of getting into the minds of the people he wrote about, hearing pieces of imaginary conversations they once carried on. This amused him, and he would share such thoughts with his brother on the evenings they spent together.

In one of these brotherly chats, Max told Felix about two knights sitting in a castle, downing endless cups of good Rhine wine and, talking about everything in the world, especially about the daughter of a neighborhood squire who had been burned at the stake as a witch. Max played both parts in this scene and could still hear Felix's loud burst of laughter when he made one of the knights say: "Just think that such a thing could happen now, in the thirteenth century!"

He was never sure if Felix's interest in history was real or just part of his love for his brother. He did know, however, that he did himself have a genuine interest in his brother's field, astronomy. Not only because he had a justifiable pride in his brother's immense scientific success but, more importantly, because everything his brother told him was also a kind of history for him. A history much much more ancient than anything a human being could ever discover from the annals of the only populated planet we know. From a cosmic perspective, this earthly chronicle looked completely different from what was measured by archeological digs or manuscripts of people who lived at various times. Human history could only establish the sequence of rulers and the rise and fall of empires but, when it came to the arrangement and rules of development, you simply had to guess. In the world of the stars, however, where Felix was at home, everything was determined precisely and could be calculated like a machine where every cog fit exactly into every wheel.

At that time it occurred to Max that what we call human history does in fact happen when our planet earth is in a certain position in the cosmos that can be calculated from its relation to the other stars. So maybe all our history is really nothing but a part of the history of the entire universe — or vice versa. Felix used to laugh at him when he began bringing home books on Indian, Persian, and God knows what other kinds of astrology.

"You already look like an old fortune teller," he said. "You better watch out or they'll burn you at the stake, like that witch you told me about."

Well, they didn't burn him at the stake, not even when they burned millions of others. He managed to live through hell — just like me — in the court of almighty Major Kohl. And maybe he survived because he believed in the stars when they told him that those born under the sign of Gemini would get through even the worst.

"I have to marry you off fast before you go completely crazy," Felix would laugh. Even though he was eight years older, he never even considered marriage for himself.

Every now and then, one of them would try to prod the other into marriage; every now and then, one of them would remind the other of how Martha used to urge them, beg them, to go out and enjoy themselves before they crumbled into dust like dry leaves — but neither of them took any of that very seriously. The house was run by an honest, good, neat old woman who kept it spotlessly clean and knew the location of every spoon and every button, who went about her work quietly and diligently and made sure they had everything they needed. The brothers never had to worry about anything. Her name was Frau Engel, but even without such a name, they would have believed she was indeed a messenger from heaven. They really didn't need anything else.

I don't know much about the older brother, but Max was satisfied with fleeting love affairs here and there. He usually came across the girls in the library, where they were working like him, or they were students he discovered amid the tomes he found for them. None of these romances lasted more than a few weeks or a couple of months at most. All of them ended in a friendly way, and afterward he never had anything to be ashamed of or to regret. None of them meant more to him than a pleasant walk in a flower garden or a lovely day or a beautiful dream or a view he had never seen before.

Just one was different. Her name was Hilde. She also worked in the university library, but everything about her was different from all he had ever known. Max told me about her so often and in such elaborate detail that I was sure I could pick her out in a crowd and know in advance what she would say even if I never laid eyes on her. But the only thing I'm going to tell you is that the year Max Himmelfarb lived with her was the happiest time of his life. Because what I know about Hilde and that year when they were together was told to me with such chaste purity that I would feel like a traitor if I told you any more.

For the first time someone brought him out of the world of books into real life, out of being stuck in the past into living in the present and dreaming of the future. For the first time he took familiar things into his hands not only to pick them up and carry them from place to place but to touch them, turn them over, examine them from all sides and be amazed at the wisdom that had created them, everything with its own special purpose. For the first time in his life, he found the beauty and wisdom of the ages in objects, in every hammer and shovel, every chair and table, every drill and ladder. For the first time he felt that someone was teaching him to stand firm with both feet on the ground — on this earth, which was suddenly so beautiful and where he loved everything now for he himself was full of love for the first time.

Then one morning, after a lovely night, he came to work and found on his desk a piece of paper with one word in big block letters: RASSENSCHAENDER.* Underneath was a drawing of a figure hanging on a gallows.

For a moment, he couldn't believe his eyes. Could it be? Here, in the university? He suddenly remembered the two knights he had joked about with Felix: "Just think that such a thing could happen now, in the thirteenth century!"

He had never been interested in politics. Naturally, he read the papers, but it was like reading raw material that

*race violator

would turn into history some day and not something that concerned him directly. Old man Bald, Hilde's father, who worked as a typesetter in a big printing press, also told him stories, but he didn't take them very seriously either. Bald was an intelligent man who read the Bible, a simple, honest man, the kind you find among typesetters more than any other group of workers. From time to time, frowning, Bald would talk about relations among the workers in the plant where he was working. Once the social democrats used to squabble with the Communists, but now there was bloodshed between them and the Nazis. Naturally, Max thought that the Nazis should never have been allowed to become so strong, but the idea that this insane house painter and his loud rabble in high boots could ever take over the government was absolute nonsense.

His eyes wandered over the library shelves. Goethe, Schiller, Kant—dozens, hundreds, of great names, perhaps the greatest in the world. It was simply absurd to think even for a moment that this nation would ever let itself be led by a mob of uneducated lunatics. Those names all around him on the shelves were his heritage too. He and his father and his grandfather before him had lived among these men; he was rooted in what they had given the world, rooted more deeply than in anything else. And yet, his eyes always came back to the piece of paper on the desk in front of him.

He couldn't concentrate on his work. He didn't know what he should do. Should he just rip it up and throw it in the trash? Or perhaps he should go to the head librarian and ask him to investigate the issue? For a moment, he thought he should show it to Hilde. Finally, he shoved it in his pocket and, even though he saw Hilde a few times during the day, he didn't mention it at all. He tried to keep it to himself. Of course Hilde knew something was bothering him and insisted on knowing why he was in such a bad mood, but he tried to find excuses and to change the subject. He said that it wasn't necessary to burden her with every silly thing and that he had to deal with this himself. But nothing helped, and ultimately the only thing left to do was pull the damned piece of paper out of his pocket and show her what was upsetting him.

She stopped under a street lamp to see the note, and he saw a wave of pain, indignation, fear, and rage wash over her face. Until the tears in her eyes drowned everything in one great grief.

"That's bad, *Junge*," she said at last. "Very bad." Then, after a long silence: "We'd better talk this over with Father."

"Do we really have to bother him with such nonsense?"

"Father's smart. And stop calling it nonsense."

Even Father Bald's intelligence didn't help much. They sat in the circle of light shed by the lamp over the white tablecloth. For a long time, the old man scratched his walrus whiskers with his bony fingers, but all he finally said was: "There are things we all have to decide for ourselves. Hilde has a head on her shoulders and whatever she decides will be what's right." Then he put on his cap, said good night to them as always, and left for the night shift.

That night, they made love as never before. But also that night, she began to part from Max.

Memories of that night and all that followed went on stinging him like a swarm of angry bees. He tried to fight the swarm, to get rid of it, but the bees came back again and again, ruthlessly, like stubborn invaders. He kept hearing Hilde pleading with him to believe one thing and one thing only—that she wasn't thinking of herself.

He heard his own voice trying to convince her that the whole thing was nothing but a nightmare and Hilde repeating over and over: "No, my dear, no. What we've lived so far was a dream. The loveliest dream. And now we're waking up into the most awful reality."

The next day she came to tell him she had requested a transfer to another branch of the library nearer her house. He still felt her hand in his and he still heard her whisper, "Don't forget, *Junge*."

The air between them seemed to quiver. He followed her with his eyes until she disappeared in the labyrinth of bookshelves. Not once did she turn around.

But he did see her one more time. It was on the day both brothers were fired from their positions in the most humiliating way, he from the library and Felix from the faculty. Helpless, like trees uprooted, overwhelmed by the torrent of blows that suddenly threatened from all sides, they felt like trapped animals. Children straying in a dark forest— they groped like blind men and found no way out. Whenever one of them came up with a glimmer of hope or an idea, another wave of doubt surged up like a thick wall and cast them back into despair.

Their heads in their hands, they were sitting silently at the table when they heard the doorbell ring. For a moment, they were petrified with fear since they knew the meaning of such a late-night visit in those days. Finally Max forced himself to get up and go open the door.

"Hilde," he whispered, for his voice failed him at that moment. She came in without a word, just looked into his eyes with a sad smile, and quickly shut the door. All he could do was repeat her name over and over.

"No, my dear," she said when he tried to help her off with

her coat. "Let's not go any further. I won't even kiss you. I know myself. I know how weak I am. I need more strength than I have to tell you why I came. I came to plead with you," she said, and all the supplications that couldn't fit into her words found room in her eyes. "Go away. You have to get out. Get out of the country. Far away. The farther the better. Please, please, do it fast, as soon as you can. I've never asked you for anything before. But now I do. In the name of all that was between us, all that still is between us, I beg you, I implore you, escape from here while there's still time."

For a long moment of silence, she looked into his eyes. Then, as if she wanted to tear herself out of a dream, she ran to the door but stood still for a moment holding the handle.

"Don't go. Stay with me," he tried to stop her.

"We mustn't, *Junge*. There's nothing I want more, but we mustn't. If I stay now, I won't be able to go. And then you won't be able to go either."

"So, let's go together."

"You know I can't. I have to stay with Father. And anyway my place is here, I know that. But your place is somewhere else."

"Where?"

"I don't know. Somewhere else. Far away from everything I'm scared of here."

He knew her better than anyone else. He knew that if she thought something through, nothing could move her. He preferred not to put into words what was going through his mind at that moment. Her hand on the doorknob, she turned to him one more time. Their eyes met for a moment and the spark that sprang up was stronger than they were. She threw herself into his arms and kissed him for the last time with all the love that was in her. Then she tore herself away from him and, as he stood there petrified, he still heard her on the other side of the closed door, running away down the stairs, far away, never to return.

Even then the Himmelfarb brothers still couldn't get rid of the feeling that everything was simply some sort of temporary lunacy. For weeks they staggered between despair and hope but didn't come up with anything remotely like a practical plan. The world around them was collapsing according to the laws of gravity while their hesitation was like a pendulum stuck on the same spot, whose range grows shorter from day to day.

Later on, in the court of the almighty Major Kohl, everything Max told me about those days was veiled in fog. Except for one thing that he still saw clearly and described to me like this:

Again the bell rings and again he goes to open the door. Six butchers in brown uniforms burst into the apartment, their legs like pillars in high boots kick and trample everything in their reach, their fists like hammers smash whatever comes to hand. First, words that stink like garbage, then quickly blows, and he and Felix are snatched up, pushed down the stairs, kicked, and in the street where there isn't a living soul, tossed into a waiting car that speeds off.

They stand with their arms up and their faces against a wall until, hours later, exhausted, they are taken for interrogation. First Felix. Not until much later did Max learn that his brother had been beaten to death that very day. He didn't know that when his turn came.

Another butcher sits at a desk that looks too small for him, like a child who has outgrown his kneepants, and every word he spits out of his mouth hits Max in the face. After every answer to questions that grow more absurd by the minute, he opens the dam and lets loose a flood of filth and curses. The objects on the desk in front of him jump as he pounds it angrily with his heavy fist.

The last thing Max Himmelfarb still sees is how the man behind the desk looms up like a mountain, takes in his heavy paw a hardbound black book, leans forward, and crashes it down on Max's head with all his might.

Then Max hears himself saying, as if from a great distance, "So, even for you, books are good for something."

He didn't see or hear anything else. He passed out. As he told me later, those were probably the only brave words that ever came out of his mouth.

But after that book had come crashing down on his head, he often had the feeling that the course of his conversation was like a train thrown off its rails.

*7

Thanks to the quick thinking of the dwarf Leo Riesenberg, everything went well for Max on the night I told you about. But there were many bad nights ahead for us, and whenever we entered the big room where Camp Commandant Kohl entertained his guests, we could never be sure we'd get out of there alive and in one piece. I'll spare you the tales of most of those nights, but I have to tell you about one of them because without it this whole story of the four court jesters wouldn't make any sense.

The juggler Adam Wahn was better trained than the rest of us for his role as entertainer and had more than one job. He wasn't there only to entertain Kohl's guests. People coming into the camp were given soap and a towel so they'd believe they were going to the showers, and they stood in a long line stretching from the entrance to the bath from which no one ever returned. As they stood in line, an orchestra of prisoners played waltzes and polkas and marches—only much later did we understand that the real purpose of that orchestra was to drown out the shouts of fear and pain of those who understood too late that they had been lured into the trap of the gas chamber. Wahn's job was to walk along the line and amuse them with his artistry. He would toss two, four, six, seven colored billiard balls, one after another, catch them as they fell, and throw them up again. The people standing in line, who still hadn't figured out that their death was waiting for them, admired his skill and couldn't take their amazed eyes off the colored billiard balls spinning in the precise orbit set by the juggler's clever hands.

Another of Wahn's jobs was teaching the camp commandant to do tricks so he could entertain the officers by pulling ping pong balls out of their ears and noses, rising to artistic heights by drawing a couple of them out of someone's trousers. They laughed hilariously as he extracted one brassiere after another from somebody's pocket.

You couldn't imagine a party at Kohl's without his four court jesters, especially the dwarf with the ridiculous name and the unbelievably clever juggler. There were always lots of women there, but in the end they were boring. Wahn, however, could always invent some new trick, and Kohl took special care of him as if he were one of the finest items in a valuable collection. He showed him off to all his friends, and the leftovers he threw the juggler as a prize for his labors would have been enough for Wahn to live through at least one more war.

Whenever Wahn tossed up the colored billiard balls, caught them and sent them off again with a twisting motion of his clever fingers, Kohl couldn't take his eyes off him. He was constantly amazed at the precision of the orbit. For hours, he would watch Wahn's hands as if he were enchanted, stare in wonder at the billiard balls spinning like a clock that stopped only at Wahn's command. Nothing in the world could bring the twirling balls to a halt except the juggler's decision that the time had come to amuse the camp commandant with some other trick.

More than once, Kohl had tried to disturb the juggler in the middle, shake his confidence, make him lose his balance and miss one of the falling billiard balls, stop him for a split second so his hand wouldn't catch one of them in time. He would talk to Wahn during the performance, force him to answer, hoping to break his concentration. He would walk back and forth and suddenly jump up next to Wahn. But the juggler's hands never stopped working like a precise machine. Kohl would even turn out the light but, when he turned it on again, Wahn would still be standing in the very same spot and the billiard balls would be spinning in the very same orbit.

This led Kohl to come up with the idea that Wahn could be good for something more than simply amusing his guests. Kohl could also use him to earn a tidy sum of money, just as a successful racehorse can make his owner rich.

At one of the next soirées, when everyone had drunk a little too much, Kohl made a solemn announcement that he was willing to take any bet that no one could succeed, by any means at all, in making the juggler lose his balance and drop even one billiard ball. The guests started betting, raised the ante and, at last, when Kohl ordered Wahn to begin the show and the billiard balls went spinning around in their orbit, they began vying with one another, inventing new ways to shake Wahn's confidence and bring this human machine that threatened to cost them a lot of money to a halt.

First they tried everything Kohl himself had already attempted. They jumped up close to Wahn all of a sudden and did everything they could to surprise him and make him lose his balance. They tried to scare him by standing in back of him and shouting in his ear. They cursed him and insulted him. They staggered by him like drunkards and made believe they would fall on top of him at any moment. But nothing in the world could make Wahn lose control of a single one of the billiard balls in its orbit.

Major Kohl applauded and piled up his winnings. Wahn didn't budge an inch, not even when one bettor pulled out his pistol and shot twice at the ceiling. Not even when Captain Walz—who was known to shoot people just for crossing his path the way other men crush cockroaches—stood in front of him with his legs spread and aimed a pistol at the juggler's heart. The billiard balls went on spinning around Walz's outstretched arm and around the barrel of the pistol with the same constant rhythm.

Then came the turn of a young lieutenant who decided to try something different. He was convinced that a man could withstand anything in the world—cold and heat, hunger and thirst—but that he couldn't resist a woman's body. And God only knows when the last time that filthy, stinking Jew had slept with a woman. Let's see what the sight of a piece of white flesh will do to his nerves.

Lieutenant von Schlangenfeld walked across the room to

a red plush sofa where a few drunken women were sprawled. Von Schlangenfeld picked out one who seemed to have the best bosom, stood her up in front of Wahn and ripped off the piece of shimmering silk that covered her body.

There she stood in front of the juggler, stark naked, and the lieutenant commanded her to make certain movements. She lifted her full breasts with the hard nipples and let them fall back like heavy grapefruits. She twisted her belly in slow rhythm, thrust out and pulled back the hairy black triangle underneath and, following von Schlangenfeld's orders, she lay down on the soft rug at Wahn's feet and opened her naked thighs so he had to see the red seal that broke at the opening of the letter he surely remembered and surely wanted to read again.

Everyone watched the performance going on before their eyes as if they were bewitched. Their eyes wandered from the naked body to the hands of the juggler and then back to the breasts and belly of the girl, who didn't do a bad job of it. At that moment, there wasn't a man among them who didn't want to pick up the woman and carry her off. Only Wahn's face stayed frozen and unmoving, his hands didn't shake a bit and went on tossing and catching the seven colored billiard balls with the precision and regularity of a machine. Although Lieutenant von Schlangenfeld had enormous powers of invention, they weren't infinite and, when he began to repeat his orders, Major Kohl decided to put an end to the game.

"*Meine Herrn*," he said, "I think that's enough for now. I promise to give you another chance. Now let's turn our attention to the ladies before they begin complaining that we're neglecting them." He signaled to the juggler and

Wahn collected his billiard balls one by one. He gathered them all and waited for further orders.

Just then, a new idea sprang up in Captain Walz's mind. He seemed to take his losses harder than the others, who were already busy dipping their hands into the dresses of the giggling girls. Suddenly, they heard the Captain say:

"With your permission, Herr Kommandant, if Herr Kommandant has no objections, I'd like to try my luck one more time later on." This time he was ready to raise his bet and asked only that the juggler wait in the next room for a few minutes.

Kohl wasn't terribly thrilled by the idea. The game was beginning to bore him but, since he had made such a handsome sum, it wouldn't have been nice to deny Walz the chance he asked. Besides, even if his winnings were big enough for one night, shouldn't he try to double them?

"All right," he said, "I'll give you one more chance on the condition that you take my bet." And he took everything he had won that evening out of his pocket, counted the money and put it on the table.

"Agreed," said Walz. While Wahn was taken to one of the adjoining rooms reserved for the officers, Walz called his orderly and whispered something in his ear. The soldier saluted and rushed out to fulfill his commander's order.

We other three court jesters sat with Wahn on the floor in a corner of the adjoining room. Before we were called back to go on with our show, the juggler had enough time to think. He knew very well that everything he had gone through up to now was nothing but child's play compared to what Walz—more cruel than all the devils in Kohl's hell—had in store for him. He didn't even try to guess what might have evolved in the mind of that executioner, but he did know that whatever it was would have been concocted in Satan's own kitchen.

He knew only one thing and kept on repeating it to himself over and over—that the only important thing was to live. To live, to live, to survive, to stay alive, to breathe. Nothing else was important to him now. Adam Wahn would not be killed. If he had to crawl, he'd crawl. If they ordered him to eat shit, he'd eat it and even say that it tasted good. Adam Wahn wanted to live. He knew he'd stay alive as long as he was useful to almighty Major Kohl. If, to be useful, he had to turn himself into an immovable robot, nothing would make him move. Adam Wahn would survive.

At last, we could all return to the big room where Kohl's party was being held. Our place was under the long table with the commandant's two dogs.

Everyone was back in their seats. The girls on the red plush sofa were arranging their skirts, but it was obvious that the officers already had other business on their minds and were expecting something truly out of the ordinary. They had an advantage over Wahn since they knew what awaited him. Where Lieutenant von Schlangenfeld had recently stood in his unsuccessful attempt to throw Wahn off balance, Walz now stood with legs akimbo and arms folded like an executioner waiting for the moment to drop the axe.

At a sign from Kohl, the juggler began to toss and catch his seven colored billiard balls, one after another, in their fixed orbit.

Then the door opened, and in its dark frame Wahn's wife appeared. Naked.

Walz knew it was likely that one of Wahn's relatives would be in the women's camp on the other side of the barbed wire fence. Mother, sister, wife, daughter—it didn't make any difference who was still there. Just so he found one of them to win his bet. His orderly did a good job. He got a prize. He found Wahn's wife and, naturally, that was better than coming back with some old woman or little child. And, without those rags, she didn't look too bad. That stinking Jew must occasionally have slipped her some of the leftovers he got from Kohl's cook. Captain Walz would put an end to all that, but tonight it was better for his purpose that she didn't look like all the others. He couldn't use a skeleton covered with yellow skin tonight.

Let's see, Walz said to himself, let's see if this stinking Jew who had already cost him so much money would be so calm this time. Not a bad idea, he thought to himself, and gave a signal to bring in the juggler's wife.

Trembling with fear and shame, she stood in front of Wahn. Their eyes met for one moment. He could see her despair and she could read the message in his eyes: This too shall pass, nothing is important now but to survive, to stay alive. Then she lowered her eyes and stood there like a statue, without moving, just like Wahn's face, not revealing a trace of what was going on inside. The colored billiard balls went up and were caught in the juggler's steady and clever hands, circled now in the narrow space between Adam Wahn and his wife.

"Look into his eyes," commanded Walz. "And you look here."

He pulled out his pistol and touched the nipples of Esther's breast with its cold barrel. She began to sob but Adam Wahn told himself that he could look without seeing, listen without hearing, and the colored billiard balls went on spinning in the same circle, not bigger, not smaller, not faster, not slower.

All that could be heard in the deathly silence of the room were Esther's sobs and the dry smack of the billiard balls landing in Wahn's hands before he threw them back up in the air. It was as if he had two minds: one of them was thinking about nothing but his wife while the other directed the clockwork precision of his movements and the juggler's long fingers didn't tremble even for a moment.

If anyone was nervous about this game, it was Captain Walz. Drops of sweat suddenly appeared on his brow, his face flushed red as a rooster's comb and, holding his pistol to Esther's breast in his right hand, he used his left to unbutton the high collar of his uniform which had become too tight for his neck, swollen now with excitement and rage.

There were times when it looked as if Walz had lost his self-control and we were sure that, in those moments, a voice in Wahn's head must have told him: Now, now, right now, take one of these spinning billiard balls and smash this mad dog's head with it. But there was also another voice that drowned out everything else and that kept repeating that the only important thing was to live, to live, and every billiard ball that was tossed and caught kept repeating: Live, live, live. And even now, nothing moved in Wahn's face.

Furious over the juggler's obvious calm and over the fact that the satanic idea he was so proud and confident of didn't work, hadn't thrown Wahn off balance, Walz began to scream, to curse, to rage, to fume. He put his pistol on Esther's temple and threatened to shoot her like a mad dog. But Adam Wahn continued unmoved, kept the seven billiard balls in their orbit and, every time he caught one as it fell and tossed it back up, he heard it whisper: Live, live, live.

Suddenly a shot was heard and none of the screams that filled the room came from Esther who dropped dead on the floor before any sound could climb out of her throat to her lips where a thin stream of blood now flowed over her white face.

"Enough!" shouted Kohl and Walz's face was pale as death. "Enough!" The commandant banged his fist on the table. "Every game has rules. That, Herr Kapitän, was in bad taste and you'll pay for it."

Enough. Adam Wahn heard the word that had always been a signal for him to stop his performance. But no, not today. That could also be a trap. No, he could not stop. He had to survive. Adam Wahn would stay alive. Live, live, live, he repeated to himself over and over and went on tossing the colored billiard balls, up, up, up, catching them and tossing them up again, catching and tossing, one after another, in the orbit he set for them.

The dead woman was taken out. Captain Walz left, deathly pale, and so did the other guests with lame and embarrassed excuses. Until, at last, except for the three court jesters cowering under the table, only the camp commandant and the juggler remained in the room. Major Kohl tried to stop Wahn several times, but he went on with his performance as if he didn't hear. Finally the major couldn't bear it any longer and left the room. Then there was only the juggler and the seven colored billiard balls still moving in a circle and Adam Wahn felt as if he were spinning with them and, at the end of every orbit, he repeated to himself: Live, live, live. Survive. Stay alive.

Under the table the dwarf hugged one of the dogs and wept like a baby. Along with Max Himmelfarb, we carried the half-crazed juggler back to the barracks and stayed awake with him all night.

8

Never were we closer to God than in those years we spent in hell. All of us.

Some people even believed that everything we witnessed had a place in God's plan. They accepted everything humbly as preordained fate and never stopped praising God's wisdom.

For a while, I slept next to a thin, simple tailor from Lodz. When he wasn't praying, he sang the same song to himself over and over in a high, thin voice. The song was in Yiddish but it began with words I could understand:

"Gott in seinem mishpat is gerecht,
Man kan nisht sagen Gott is shlecht..."

"God is just . . . One cannot say that God is bad. . ." I don't remember much beyond that. He usually hummed the rest of it as if he were trying to rock himself to sleep. But one more sentence from that song sticks in my memory:

"Gott weiss was er tut.
Umƶist straft er keinen nisht. "

"God knows what He does. No one is punished in vain." Nothing could shake the faith of the tailor from Lodz, Efraim Grien. The last time I heard the song—and the tune still rings in my ears—it was on the other side of the wall where a Kapo threw him out of the barracks for some minor infraction of the rules. They ordered him to kneel in the snow and ice, and he sang. At first, his voice was louder than ever, then it grew weaker and weaker until it finally stopped, and the silence was loudest of all. In the morning, we had to hack his dead body out of the ice with an axe.

Many of us in Major Kohl's hell never wavered in our belief. And there were others who turned to God not because they believed but because they were groping for something in that darkness. They prayed and begged, promised and swore, took vows. Even those who didn't believe spoke to God in that hell, just like everybody else. The only thing that distinguished them from the believers was that their prayers began with, "If You exist. . ."

God was mother's skirt, the place where you're safe, the tree you touch when you're playing tag so they can't catch you—like the altar in a sanctuary. God was a refuge, a harbor for a ship in a storm, a straw for a drowning man. Everyone turned to God, everyone talked to Him. Some of them all the time, some of them often, others only in the hardest times. But everyone wanted to be close to Him at least once.

I used to turn to Him, too. I too begged for answers and there were even moments when I thought I understood His signs. Everything had a reason, a purpose, a destiny. I even believed that my deformity had a place in God's higher plan. In the mosaic of billions of little stones, I must have been put in just the right place. I seemed to hear Him say that, just because of that sacrifice, He could give me something he couldn't give to others, a talent not everyone could have. Even later, when I couldn't understand anymore, I still believed that God must have had some special purpose—at least for those who survived, like the four court jesters of Major Kohl. Maybe He chose us to serve as witnesses for all the evil that man is capable of doing.

And I know the precise moment when even that last trace of my faith deserted me.

Three days earlier I had paid off my debt. If Kohl had saved our lives by protecting his four court jesters, I now saved his. I'll never be sure if what I did was right, but it was what I did.

"You know that the Russians are getting close," I said to him when I was allowed to speak. "They'll be here in forty-eight hours. You'll survive but only if you leave right away and don't waste any time."

I knew how dangerous it was to be the bearer of bad tidings. In a sudden rush of rage, he could have shot me on the spot. He could have had all of us slaughtered and been rid of any witnesses. But I also knew that Kohl used to sit by the radio for hours, so he couldn't have really been surprised at what I told him. I, on the other hand, had no access to a radio and Kohl must have been absolutely certain I would never have dared put my neck in a noose for I knew very well what the punishment was if I were caught listening to one. Clearly, then, my warning didn't come from enemy news broadcasts. It must have come from another source and perhaps what Kohl needed was just such a confirmation. He even nodded as if to thank me.

At night they locked us up with all the others in the cages of the huts. Even now they could have burned down the buildings they herded us into. None of us could sleep that night, not even the most exhausted. Max Himmelfarb lay next to me again and repeated God knows how many times: "Don't worry. Gemini will survive." I don't know if he repeated that to keep up my spirits or his own.

We held our breath and listened to the sounds of the night. We heard orders shouted angrily but couldn't make out their meaning. We heard confused running around, guards cursing, dogs barking, motors starting up, and, finally, the sound of the trucks leaving.

Two days later, when the first Russian troops reached the camp, they didn't find a single German. They found dozens of sacrifices to death. But death wasn't yet satisfied, for when the skeletons made a banquet of what was left in the abandoned warehouses, it turned out to be the last meal for many of them.

But the four of us survived, and, after a night march, we sat at dawn in a train, waiting in a station crowded with people like us who had come from the liberated camps and were following the advancing armies westward.

We all looked the same. All of us with the striped rags of camp inmates hanging on our bones. Here and there someone had managed to get hold of a pair of trousers or boots or a shirt, and that made him a rich man in our eyes.

Wherever we turned, we encountered the sharp edges of things we were all trying to forget, each of us in his own way. Many people made cigarettes of the newspaper and cheap tobacco they got from the Russian soldiers. They would look at the smoke rising from their cigarettes and try to read tomorrow and the day after in the blue and gray clouds over their heads. The train was full of dreams. Some people looked out the open windows and their eyes, moving back and forth from one end of the sky to the other, from stone to stone, from tree to tree, couldn't begin to satisfy their hungry senses. The air they breathed was full of smoke and soot and reeked of toilets and gasoline, but they took it into every corner of their lungs for it was the air of freedom.

Others sat withdrawn into themselves as if they were counting their losses, sifting through the ashes. As if they were looking into an open grave and only now could grasp the full horror of what they had gone through. The ditch suddenly began to stretch into a bottomless abyss.

But most of them were simply trying to drown out whatever it was inside them that asked, whatever it was that filled them with fear and uncertainty, whatever it was that tore their hearts with the premonition of the emptiness awaiting them at the end of the voyage. They shouted at one another with artificial, tense cheer; they traded jokes back and forth, mostly vulgar ones; here and there a half-forgotten song burst out of a throat that couldn't remember the last time it sang. The voices in the weak bodies were also weak but there were so many of them that when one joined with another, they gathered strength like a river overflowing its banks.

In our corner of the car, the dwarf Leo Riesenberg talked

more than anyone else. His surprisingly strong voice drowned out all the others. The court jesters of the once almighty Major Kohl remained together even now, on their way to freedom. The stargazer and the juggler and I had no desire to talk, but the dwarf with the funny name that made you think of a lion on a gigantic mountain kept up a steady stream of thoughts gushing out of his head like water out of a fountain.

He stood on the bench to be sure we were listening to him and began in his usual way: "Gentlemen, gentlemen, here—" and he pointed with his childlike finger to his disproportionately large head on his thin body with short legs—"here, gentlemen, everything is thought out to the very last detail. And you there, you *better* listen too! It won't hurt you to hear the words of a wise man."

That was directed to the four other skeletons in striped rags who were crowded into the compartment with us. They had gotten hold of a deck of cards somewhere and were now so absorbed in their game that the most eloquent speech wouldn't have drawn their attention. Leo Riesenberg merely made a small gesture to indicate that it was a hopeless case and went on.

"Gentlemen, our strength lies in organization. Dwarfs of the world, unite! Gentlemen, a million dwarfs. Do you have any idea what kind of strength there is in that? Do you understand what power that represents? It would be enough for one dwarf to hide under the table at every government meeting in the world—and there's nothing easier—and we'll have all the secrets of the world. Gentlemen, do you understand what that means? Who will be able to thwart the plans of the next Hitler? We will, gentlemen, we dwarfs."

As he talked, he thumped his breast with his tiny hand, imitating the speeches of the popular orators we knew from before the war. Obviously, he wanted to make us laugh, but at times it was hard to tell what was supposed to be funny and what was serious since he was moving dangerously close to the sharp edge of truth.

"For thousands of years, the earth has been ruled by giants and those who thought they were giants. And what did they give us? What? I ask you, gentlemen, what did they achieve? And I say — enough! Now, gentlemen, give us dwarfs a chance. And once again, I call on you, gentlemen, dwarfs of all sizes, unite! You're six feet? Six three? Too bad. What a waste of cloth for your coat and trousers, what a waste of leather for your shoes. Never mind. The important thing is that you all know that you're dwarfs and not giants. Take Goliath, for example. That was his whole problem, he didn't know how small he was. But David did know he was bigger than he looked. The giants, gentlemen, are the ones who brought us to the bottom of the pit that the human brain is capable of imagining for itself. No, deeper than that. Now let the smallest ones get to the top. Join the dwarf party. We've gone down with the giants and the big bosses. Now, gentlemen, let's get up and rise higher and higher with the dwarfs.

"One more thing, gentlemen," he went on in a shrill voice, going up and down the scale and back again. And, at the same time, he was hopping back and forth on his short legs and seemed to be standing in a swaying boat that threatened to tip over any minute. "Gentlemen, every one of us must make his own unique contribution. And I, gentlemen, have already prepared my own project. We're going to set up a circus of dwarfs. Manager, Leo Riesenberg, 4 feet 3 inches tall, has the honor to invite you, gentlemen, to the gala premiere. Do you know how sublime that will be? Just imagine, gentlemen, imagine. The great Leo Riesenberg, a lion of lions. The only dwarf wild animal tamer. And what an animal tamer! The world, gentlemen, has never seen anything like it. And now, gentlemen," he concluded, "now, gentlemen, here's to the success of the dwarf circus, to you and your health, I'm going to pee. I hope you'll wait for me."

It never occurred to him to push his way through the crowds. He crawled out through the window, landed like a monkey on the platform where we watched him do a somersault and then rushed along the tracks. He hopped rather than walked, with short, tottering steps, his little body bent forward like a bird in a hurry and his big head constantly moving from side to side. Then he disappeared between two cars.

A few minutes later the train seemed to move. We heard the metallic sound of the steel bumpers but that didn't bother anyone. They were obviously testing the couplings, which meant we'd soon be leaving. That's what we would have said to ourselves if, just then, an agonizing shriek hadn't split the smoke-filled air and, even though it lasted only a split second, it drowned out everything else and created a coil of horror in our throats.

On the ledge between two cars, we found Leo Riesenberg's delicate little body crushed. Even the puddle of blood he lay in was small.

After all we had been through in the years just ended, after all we had been witness to, nothing much had happened here now. The world was simply poorer by one Jewish dwarf. And maybe by a couple of dreams too. But from that moment on, I never addressed God again.

9

We buried little Leo Riesenberg in a field near the tracks and, for endless hours, the three of us who were left were carried in a train away from the hell we knew toward the unknown, which we approached with a mixture of fear and hope. Yet as the train stopped at every single station—and it seemed as if there were hundreds of them—we felt the hope shrinking smaller and smaller and the fear of the emptiness waiting for us growing bigger and bigger.

At one of those stations the juggler Adam Wahn left us. We simply shook hands, and he left without saying a word. I gave him a piece of paper with an address where letters would surely get to me, but he just shrugged his shoulders and didn't wait for the train to leave and didn't even wave goodbye to us. He merely disappeared in the crowd on the platform.

Then, after traveling for several hours, it was my turn to leave the train and confront the darkness ahead of me. Now Max Himmelfarb went on alone, not yet knowing that he was only going from one hell to another. And I couldn't even tell him since what they used to call my clairvoyance had apparently deserted me after I used it to perform the last service for the once almighty camp commandant Major Kohl.

Max also had my address but, as with Adam Wahn, no letter ever came from him either. The two letters I sent to him through general delivery in his hometown came back undelivered a few months later so I didn't find out about his second hell until we met years later in Jerusalem.

Anywhere else, I would have called it an accidental meeting, but in this city there are no accidents.

It turned out that he had been living in Jerusalem for some years, having left his hometown soon after he had arrived back there. During his short stay in Germany, before he left forever, as during the years in Jerusalem before we met again, there were many reasons why he had never tried to get in touch with me or anyone else he had known in the past. But now he was beside himself with joy. I had to go with him to his room in one of those old houses on a little street off Jaffa Road, and it was long past midnight when he walked me back home to my house in the street that leads to Jaffa Gate. (In those days, the street really didn't lead to Jaffa Gate but to a high wall that divided Jerusalem into two cities.) The entire time Max didn't stop telling me everything that had happened to him since the day the train carried us into the dark emptiness. First all four of Major Kohl's court jesters, then only three, then two and then Max all alone, returning to his hometown, or at least to what the war had left of it.

The house he had grown up in was nothing but a pile of rubble. However, he did find the old housekeeper, Frau Engel, in her own little house where she had returned after she couldn't work for the Himmelfarb brothers anymore. (Even then, she had still come secretly once a week to clean up and keep everything straight.) By some miracle, her house had been spared in all the air raids and now stood out in that sea of ruins like a tooth in empty gums.

The good old woman fell into his arms and began to cry and repeat over and over, "At least one of you came back!" She ran all around the room looking for something to feed him and restore his strength.

Although he had already known for a long time that Felix was no longer alive, somewhere deep inside he still had a glimmer of hope—not to hope was too awful. All those years he had convinced himself that what he heard from other prisoners who saw Felix killed could have been a mistake. Only now did he know that he had been fooling himself. Now, after he had lost the last flicker of hope, he needed Hilde even more than ever.

Everything now drew him to her, to the simple house next to the railroad tracks where she lived with her wise father and where they had spent a year of happiness together. Everything drew him to her, but before he could set out, he had to climb a high wall of horrible fear that suddenly rose up in front of him. He was afraid. Maybe he had never known such fear as now when he was scared of what was waiting for him at the end of the journey to which every-thing drew him and which he postponed for hours and hours.

So many years had gone by. So many things could have happened in the meantime. How could she imagine that, out of all those thousands, he would come back alive from that hell? Wasn't it likely she had gotten married meanwhile and that he would find her with children who, like her, belonged to some other man? And even if no one else had taken his place, love wasn't like the moon, waxing and waning. When love began to disappear, it finally evaporat-ed altogether, like the scent of a withered rose. Couldn't that have happened to their love? A hundred other things occurred to him now. What, for instance, did he know about how people here might have changed after so many years of knowing nothing but high boots marching, banners with swastikas, and *Sieg Heil*?

He knew only that he was afraid. Could he also survive that? He was scared, and he hesitated. He washed, shaved, and even dressed in one of Felix's suits that Frau Engel had been able to save in time before the house was sealed. In the end, he overcame his fear and set out, along the railroad tracks, on that road he remembered so well.

Suddenly he rushed. He had to know. Whatever had happened, he had to know. He had to be sure.

He rang the doorbell and an old woman came limping toward him. She held a cane in one hand and, with the other, shaded her eyes, which obviously were weak. Maybe it's an old relative, he thought, whom they had taken in during the war.

"Excuse me, does the Bald family still live here?" The possibility that they had moved for some reason—perhaps

Hilde had found work somewhere else—occurred to him only now.

"Who?" The old woman took her hand away from her eyes and put it to her ear. "Who? The Balds? No, sir, they don't live here anymore. They don't live anywhere anymore." She suddenly became talkative and wagged her wrinkled head. "Nobody'll visit 'em anymore. Not even in the cemetery. No one, sir. They shot 'em, piff, paff, puff!" She aimed her cane like a rifle. "Yep, they killed 'em, both of 'em. Father and daughter. They were hiding Jews here." With her bony finger, she tapped her furrowed brow.

He couldn't even thank her for the information. He turned around and ran away and didn't stop until he reached the river. There he lay on the bank in the grass where he had first kissed Hilde an eternity ago. He threw himself down and only now did weeping contort his body.

It occurred to him only later to ask: Where are all the tears that are shed in this world? How can it be that cities aren't drowned in them? That mountains are not washed away in their flow? Hadn't there been enough tears in these dreadful years to make such a deluge?

Sometime during that night, it happened for the first time—what was later to be repeated often. Rage suddenly overcame all feelings, even grief, and all the pent up fury burst out like a volcano of hatred for the One Who was almighty and could have changed things and yet looked down indifferently on all the horrors. He began to tear up clumps of grass and fling them straight at the sky.

"Good? Just? Merciful?" he shouted with every toss. "No. You're evil. Wicked. Vile. I see You behind every star. Laughing mockingly at these powerless humans."

Clumps of grass and stones fell into the river and it

sounded as if someone couldn't help laughing and clapping his hands merrily. Then he fell back onto the ground, even more desperate, and buried his face in the grass.

All night long, Max Himmelfarb stayed like that with his grief. When he finally stood up the next morning to go back to the city, only one thing was clear to him: He had to leave. No matter where, just away, far, far away from here.

10

We found one another years later, in Jerusalem. Anywhere else, I would have called it a lucky coincidence but, when I tell you how we met, I'm sure you'll agree that nothing in this city is a coincidence.

That morning, I had moved my few earthly possessions to two small rooms I had found on Mamila Street, a street that once led to Jaffa Gate and now leads there again but, at that time, it led only to the gray partition that divided Jerusalem in half.

The man who moved my things — one Ovadiah, who had come to Eretz Israel from Kurdistan with his father some fifty years before — was one of those porters who used to sit on the steps on the corner, waiting for work. "Mazel tov!

Good luck and best wishes," he said; "may you never need us to move your things to another place."

His good wishes must have helped since I've been very happy ever since on this street. It's a street full of dreams and nothing would please me more than to tell you about the dreamers and someday I will. But not now. Now I'm trying to tell you the story of the four court jesters of the once almighty Major Kohl and I mustn't dam up the flow and overflow the banks.

Opposite the steps of the moving company's office where the porters would sit, on the other corner, was a small cubicle of a kiosk. A short, stocky man, healthy and lively, with a cap on his round head, stands there behind the counter all day long. He waits on his customers with a smile and not for a moment does he stop his running commentary on events occurring on the street, in Jerusalem, in the country, and in the world. This Menachem Salz pleased me from the first moment I saw him, when I went to buy a newspaper from him the day I moved in and he gave me a few stories that didn't appear in the paper. I think we became friends right then and, really, I'd like nothing more than to tell you about Menachem. I will, I promise. But it'll have to wait, too.

At night, I went back to the kiosk, this time for a cup of tea but mostly to listen to a little more of Menachem's wisdom, and that's where it happened.

There is a moment at dusk in Jerusalem when a pink nacre begins to flow down the slope of the sky toward the horizon. It was just at the beginning of that hour when I suddenly saw him approaching the street from the other side, carrying what looked like a spear on his shoulder and a royal scepter in his hand. There could be no doubt. The thin, angular, still erect body; the thin neck that always reminded me of a bird, always sticking out a little as if it were walking one step ahead; the long head, even though I had never seen the thin, waving beard—and when he came close, the eyes, a child's eyes the color of cornflowers, in a face old before its time—all that could belong only to Max Himmelfarb. He looked like an old king who had sallied forth to do battle for justice.

He didn't see me and I was so amazed at that sudden and unexpected encounter that my throat grew parched like a dry river bed and not even the thinnest flow of words could get through. I was glad to have another moment before we shook hands.

The spear and the scepter turned out to be the tripod and the old telescope, and Max now set up the tripod under the streetlamp on the corner, fixed the telescope on it, focused it, and then looked as if he were waiting for the nacre to be replaced by purple and then turned into a meadow of cobalt full of golden flowers of the stars. Then he would search for customers. Whenever he saw anyone coming, he would begin his spiel like a mournful plea, as if he were praying for the salvation of the world:

"Stars, gentlemen. Ladies and gentlemen, stars! The moon, Venus, Mars, Orion. Look at the stars, look at the stars. They're closer than you think. The sky is open before your eyes. Don't you want to see the stars? You really don't want to see them?"

He craned his long, bird's neck at everyone who passed by, looking all the while at the stars and, each time, he would turn to Menachem standing behind the counter of his kiosk and complain:

"People don't want to look at the stars. To lift up their

eyes and look at the sky. They walk with their heads down all the time, like they're looking for something they lost. Maybe they could find it up above. What do they know?"

When I felt my throat was finally able to let my words through, I went up to the stargazer—it turns out that was what they called him here—and asked if I could look.

Now he looked at me but didn't yet seem to know who I was.

I said casually:

"You must be a Gemini."

"Gemini," he repeated and looked at me with his innocent eyes. "Gemini, Gemini," he recited, like a magic formula. Only then did he burst out with something between a roar of joy and a wail of pain. "The judge! The judge! Yes, Gemini. I told you we'd get through it together. See, I told you." Then again: "All this time, Judge, all this time. Where have you been? I knew you'd come. It was written in the stars. But so much time, Judge."

He embraced me and stroked my face and I don't know how long he held me until I heard him say in a trembling voice:

"Don't leave me again, Judge."

I promised I wouldn't and a smile spread over his face not only from side to side as on other faces but as if it stretched from north to south, from the chin to the forehead and it stayed there all night. He danced up and down and pranced all around and so did I, both of us shouting all the time. Good old Menachem Salz watched us from his kiosk, pushed back his cap and scratched his head as he always did when he heard or saw something amazing.

That night, Max Himmelfarb forgot the stars. First I took him to my new place and then I went with him to see his room on a sidestreet off Jaffa Road. Then he accompanied me home and then I went back with him and, all the time, we had something to remember and something to add about the time that seemed so long when we had been apart. We had so much to tell each other. It must have been almost dawn when we finally said goodnight.

11

It was then that I learned about Hilde and that night on the riverbank when all the grief and rage that had been piling up in him during those years in the camps and in Major Kohl's court burst out of Max Himmelfarb like lava from a volcano.

I also learned what had brought him to Eretz Israel for that was more amazing than my own story. I at least had a grandfather who lived with us and, as a small child, I used to listen to his tales and dreams about Jerusalem; but I knew that Max came from a completely assimilated family. I recalled that he had told me years before that the Judaism of the Himmelfarb family consisted merely of two visits a year to the synagogue when the Professor put on his silk top hat and sat in one of the first rows surrounded by his two sons. After the father died, the sons stopped doing even that.

The only link left to Judaism was Frau Himmelfarb's younger brother, who was a Zionist, so the rest of the family considered him a bit crazy. Uncle Samuel was a bachelor and a prosperous stockbroker in London. As long as his sister was alive, he used to come for a short visit every couple of years. When she died, he stopped coming. It wasn't until Max had emerged from one hell and was trying with all his might to escape from the second that he remembered what was probably his only living relative. He dug up the address from somewhere and kindly Uncle Samuel first brought him to London and then put him on a boat for Eretz Israel where he also planned to settle himself.

The plan was foiled by death. Samuel dropped dead suddenly without leaving a will and some distant relatives Max had never heard of claimed the inheritance. All Max had was what Samuel had given him to help him over the first few months until he himself arrived and that wasn't enough to carry out an expensive lawsuit. So he was left empty-handed.

I learned about that and about many other things that night from Max himself. Afterward, Menachem Salz added a great deal to my knowledge since he had known Max for many years before the two of us met again. Truth is, I really don't remember what I learned from which of them but that's not very important. Most of it comes down to the fact that he made a new beginning in a hard land even though he was poor and lonely and lost and, worst of all, sick.

It wasn't easy to learn the language and look for work. Then, things he tried to forget weren't easily suppressed and kept coming back and hovering in front of his eyes. He kept going over moments he tried in vain to convince himself had never happened. He wanted to believe it had all been a nightmare, that all the bloody banners waving in front of him were nothing but a bad dream.

The groans from thousands of prison cells, pits piled up with thousands of stiff corpses brought day and night in full carts, pits filled with rows and rows of people murdered with machine guns, torture chambers, gallows, graves sprinkled with lime and, at every step, Hilde's eyes looked out at him. That and so many other horrors were inscribed in him, deep, as if they were chiseled in stone, carved and no matter how he tried to repress it, he knew he had gone through it all. He knew that a piece of his own life was buried in every one of those pits and in every one of those graves.

Ever since he had been hit over the head by the uniformed butcher's apprentice but, even more—ever since the old woman had told him about Hilde's death, he couldn't get rid of the feeling that he was groping his way high up in the air like a tightrope walker and that, any moment, he was liable to fall down and be crushed. Even at the best of times, he moved as if he were walking on thin ice, uncertain and always afraid of stumbling.

I won't try to diagnose or delve deeply into Max's case. From what he told me—and his mind was always lucid enough for him to admit the fact of his illness—he was hurled between excitement about everything around him and dull apathy that often carried him along helplessly like a broken branch in the middle of the river. Fear and depression frequently led him to the doctor and, each time, he spent a few weeks in an institution. There, he would look out through a barred window at the sky above the pine trees along the fence or sit on a bench and look around. And when the day grew dark and a nurse came to wipe the tears from his eyes before she took him back to his room, only then did he know he had been weeping all the time. Sometimes, he told me, he felt that he himself was one of those shadows he saw hopping around between the dark and the light, going up and down between sky and earth. And sometimes he thought he saw so much of the suffering of others that he himself began to suffer like them.

He told me he would return from these sojourns in the sanitarium calmer and healthier, they told him, although he always felt older and weaker. But, in the last two years, he claimed, he had finally found tranquility. He tried not to think about the past and not to worry about the future. As for the future, he was always capable of earning the few pennies he needed to exist. Maybe it wasn't such a glorious profession but what did we court jesters of Major Kohl have to do with laurels? Maybe it wasn't such a prestigious way to make a living but what was wrong with developing passport pictures in the street and what was wrong with showing people the stars? What's more important than reminding people that there's something in the universe besides the planet they inhabit?

In fact, he came to that—which he had been doing for years—only after a whole string of disappointments, after he had failed in all his efforts to find work at the university or in other libraries, in editorial offices, with publishers and God knows where else. Menachem told me that, in most cases, the reason for his failure was just what I described before as a sudden gust of wind that scattered all the index cards in the catalogue of his memory.

One day, when he was coming back from the university

where he had tried unsuccessfully to get a job in the library and, before he descended from Mount Scopus, he stood for a while in the stone amphitheater. At that hour, there usually wasn't anyone there. For the first time, the panorama of the Judean Desert lay open before him like a painted fan, with a hazy wreath of the Ephraim Mountains in the background. Round sand dunes lay side by side, huddled together between white shadows like a herd resting under dark tents and, from time to time, a single bird would cross the clear sky shaking the air over the broad landscape.

He felt then—and later on, in the hard times, he felt it more than once—that the city behind him was putting its hands on his shoulders. That the light breeze from the distant mountains was stroking his brow and cheeks. And the whole landscape all around him seemed to whisper. "Yihyeh tov," it will be OK, whispered the city. "Yihyeh tov," the desert soothed him and, from the Ephraim Mountains came the same words and hovered over the mirror of the Dead Sea which he saw for the first time in the distance. Everything said: "It will be OK." Those were the first words every new immigrant learned. And though he had laughed at them earlier, on that day, at that moment, he believed in them.

When he got home to the room he rented in a side street off Jaffa Road, he dug a box out from under his bed. In it was a camera Frau Engel had saved and, though it was old-fashioned, it could still be used. He had gotten it from his father when he was a boy and he used to love playing with it. Sometimes he had even managed to make a good picture with it and now and then could capture a moment he knew would never come back again.

He wanted to be sure the camera he hadn't used for so

long was still in working order for he intended to go back to the amphitheater soon to try to capture at least something of what he had seen that day. Something of all the magic and peace of the play of light and shadow along the whole Judean Desert and the Ephraim Mountains. In short, he decided to try his luck as a photographer.

He began to work with some newspapers and even managed to sell a few pictures, but it paid so badly he couldn't cover his expenses. He made more money photographing weddings and bar mitzvahs. Later on, he started coming every morning to the building where they issued passports, drivers' licenses, and other documents. He knew that all those papers required a photograph, so he set up his tripod at the entrance and got permission to use an old van in the yard as a darkroom where he developed the negatives and made copies. You could walk around town, do some window shopping and, when you came back after an hour, your pictures were all ready.

Later, during the War of Independence in 1948, things began to take shape again in Max Himmelfarb's mind. Suddenly he was again interested in everything going on around him, he asked about everything, got information from everybody, read whatever came into his hands, took notes, arranged, classified, sifted through everything expertly even when his brain was dead tired of provable facts, of alarming rumors and, while he waited for customers who needed photos for various documents, he soon began to explain to others what was really taking place now and where the next development in the country would be.

What he said made good sense. The people who listened to him nodded, and Max knew they spread his opinions to others. Not only did it seem to him that, for the first time in several years, he was needed once again, but he also told himself that he had only now discovered his talent for explaining things to others and, someday, that talent could be put to much better and more systematic use.

At that time, people needed more than news and commentary. More than anything else, they needed hope. Then Max remembered the stars.

In the big suitcase under his bed where he kept all the treasures Frau Engel had saved from falling into the hands of those hoodlums in high boots, there was also a small telescope that had belonged to Felix. One day, Max took it out, brought it to a nearby locksmith along with the tripod, and the next day, the tripod was fitted with a new bolt to attach either the telescope or the camera. That night, he stood in front of Café Hatikva with the telescope aimed at the star-studded sky. When he succeeded in coaxing the first customer who came out of the café to look through the metal cylinder of the telescope, he was — as he told me — very happy. The camera helped him to serve people, and the telescope — to fulfill a mission. People had to know, he kept repeating, that there are things in the world beyond their own planet.

He came every night, set up his tripod and invited the customers entering or leaving the café to look at the stars. He continued to come until the café went bankrupt and closed its doors. Then he tried a few other places but either the police or the doormen threw him out and, finally, he came to the kiosk on King David Street at the corner of the street that led then and leads again today to Jaffa Gate. That very same street where I found myself a home when I came to Jerusalem.

Here, in front of the kiosk that belonged to Menachem

Salz, the good man we both became friendly with, we found one another years later and here the two remaining court jesters of the court of Major Kohl met every evening, from then on, at the hour when the pink nacre begins to flow down the slope of the sky above Jerusalem and beyond the horizon.

*12

Whenever I asked about his health, Max would assure me that he felt fine. But Menachem Salz, who was always worried about him, told me several times when we were alone about how a sudden gust of wind would still hit our friend's brain. I saw it myself a few times but it always looked like a momentary confusion that passed very quickly. In general, Max looked physically healthy and contented with his life and he divided his time between service and destiny. Even though Menachem Salz and I knew that a trace of illness still remained in Max Himmelfarb's brain, we were reconciled to the fact that it would never change. As long as the symptoms stayed as they were, we could deal with them. It was enough to pay attention to the sudden change in the topic of conversation, to be quiet for a moment and wait for Max to come back on the right track.

Things could surely have gone on like that if—as Max had once believed long ago but no more—everything was written in the stars for there was something in them that none of us could read.

One night, I felt I was coming down with the flu and went home earlier than usual. Menachem was just about to count the day's receipts, put all the perishables back in the icebox and stack the cases of empty bottles when the street suddenly echoed with a burst of unrestrained laughter approaching the corner. Hoping to find some customers, the stargazer hurried from the kiosk where he was chatting with Menachem and began to shout as always:

"Stars, gentlemen, stars! Pink Venus, red Mars! Look at the stars. You don't know how close they are."

A gang of teenagers took up the whole width of the sidewalk and ran like a pack of wild horses. They ran, they kicked up their legs, swung their bodies back and forth, shoved one another, shouted to each other and replied to everything with wild laughter. When they came to the stargazer, they formed a circle around him and began to amuse themselves at his expense. They joked uproariously and slapped each other on the back in savage joy. They contorted their bodies in laughter like drunks and, trying to outdo all the others, one of them said:

"OK, show us your stars."

He came up to the tripod, bent down over the telescope, pretended to stumble and overturned telescope and tripod—to the great amusement of the rest of them.

For a moment, Max was petrified. His lips moved but it

took a while until the words that emerged from his parched throat could be understood. Then he began to shout:

"Rowdies! Bandits! You'll pay for this! Help! Help!"

One of the teenage hooligans quickly shut him up by pressing his throat while the other one picked up the tripod and brought it down heavily on the stargazer's head. He didn't neglect to add a joke but this time he didn't get the expected burst of laughter because, when they saw the stargazer lying on the ground, they all ran for their lives.

Menachem, who told me the whole story the next morning, heard the cries for help and ran out of the kiosk just as Max took the blow and collapsed to the ground, unconscious.

Max Himmelfarb spent several weeks in the hospital with a severe concussion but the blow he got from the young ruffian turned into a blessing in disguise. Max was convinced that that blow undid the one he had received long ago from the book-loving SS man.

Afterward, he tried to describe to me the strange things that took place in his mind during those weeks in the hospital.

"Mother loved cats," he told me, "and we always had a few of them and their kittens around the house. I felt just like when they would upset Mother's sewing basket and all the needles and pins and skeins of wool and thread would fall out and get all mixed up in a hopeless tangle."

What happened yesterday was suddenly on the bottom and what happened years ago rose up to the surface of his consciousness. Like one of those drums in the lottery with all the numbers, big and small, odd and even, mixed up in a hailstorm of wild chances. What he had experienced blended with what he had only dreamed, what he had read and what he knew merged with things he had only heard somewhere or perhaps only imagined and everything had the same value and there was no difference between fact and dream, knowledge and imagination, today and yesterday. There were things the wind seemed to blow away irrevocably but there were also things he hadn't thought about since his childhood and now he lived through them again. There were other things he couldn't remember knowing and now they were suddenly clear.

"Then I saw Mother," he said. "She was smiling and she said: 'Good. Now at last we have to straighten things up as they should be.'"

Then they would sit on the floor with Mother and sort buttons in little boxes, mother-of-pearl buttons in one box, bone and metal buttons in another. They put the pins together and the needles and unraveled tangles of wool and rolled thread on their spools. Until everything was neat and in its proper place. But this time, Mother had to go somewhere and he couldn't manage so well all by himself and it took him several days and nights to do it.

He lay in a deep fog and dreamed that he was arranging items in the card catalogue of his memory which had been ruffled and blown by the wind. He put one on top of another as when he used to build houses of playing cards that collapsed every time and he'd have to start all over again. Only this time he wasn't building houses but stairways to climb higher and higher. Just when he finished with one and wanted to climb up to build higher, the stairs always collapsed beneath him and he fell down with them and was always sitting once again contemplating the same

confused bunch of strings which seemed to have no beginning and no end.

King David played on his harp of human bones before
the doors of the gas chamber, and the juggler Adam Wahn
threw colored billiard balls up to the sky, which shattered
like a window struck with a stone and, instead of stars,
unmoving toads sat in the heavens.

For several days and nights, these and other images
flitted past his eyes and many other shapes from his memory fluttered like leaves falling from autumn trees. Sometimes he seemed to be lying among them, covered as in a
grave with crumbling clumps of earth. Other times, he
seemed to be resting in a soft bed and there were also
moments he waded through fallen leaves like a small boy,
thrilled by the rustling whisper of their response when he
stroked them with his delicate steps in the November paths.

Then things began to fall into place all by themselves.
The fever went down but even now, he still had to clear his
way carefully through jungle and primeval forest, to tramp
through deserts, to sail between God knows how many
reefs. He no longer knew how many rivers were still covered with ice, how many fields were coated with snow, how
many valleys lay under fog, how many ashes had to be
buried, how many stones and pieces could be gathered
together from the piles of debris so that one stone could be
painstakingly put with another, one corner with another
and the whole thing could flow together and unite in one
shape. He only knew that, in those days and nights of dark
helplessness, he was working on something like piecing
together a shattered mirror. But he couldn't have said where
all the silver came from to cover the new base with a new

layer absorbing beams and beams of light until he could recognize himself in it.

He didn't see everything all at once. For a long time, his stimulated senses worked like a movie camera panning from one face to another, one scene to another and it took a while for the camera to record a broad vista. Nevertheless, he was beginning to be sure of himself, sure that everything would be straight once again in the card catalogue of his memory. He could leaf through it again, take out notes, read them and, for the first time, really understand what was on them and that was the biggest difference from the hours of helplessness but also from the many years before those hours.

And that's how I found Max Himmelfarb again. It was as if, after wandering around in a dark woods for a long time, he had come on a clearing where a sun-filled landscape stretched before his eyes. His senses were clearer now than I had ever known them to be. He was happy with the new work he had decided on during those weeks in the hospital when he had been looking for a way out of the labyrinth. He wanted to become a tourist guide. He felt he could be useful again and he seemed to be at peace with everything and everyone, even with himself. But even though he never gave any impression of fear and never expressed any sad thoughts, I knew him too well not to know that not all the clouds had disappeared from his sky.

*[*]13

Clouds may cover the sun, but sometimes they may also hide behind it. For years Max Himmelfarb kept the clouds of his thoughts hidden. He did this so well that even I, who was sure they had to be somewhere in the depths of his mind, couldn't find any trace of them under the calm and collected surface of his face. Naturally, we never mentioned them in our daily conversations.

Here I must add that my gift for seeing what other people can't see had left me almost completely after I came to Jerusalem. As if I didn't need it anymore. Not here. So I didn't know if I should welcome it or try to get rid of it when I felt it coming back to me years later in those weeks of tension and fear before the Six Day War in June 1967.

One night I suddenly felt as if I were taking off and hovering over the city, as if invisible wings were carrying me to the window sill of Max Himmelfarb's room in the old house on the side street off Jaffa Road.

I saw him sitting at the table, reading the newspaper. When he finished, he got undressed, folded his pants carefully along the seam, and draped them over the back of a chair. He turned out the light and lay down on his bed. But he didn't fall asleep. He looked at the dark ceiling and talked to himself: "There'll be a war," I heard him say. "There'll be a war. First the politicians will bark and then the machine guns will. First they shoot words, then bombs."

He was silent a moment as if he were waiting for an answer and then he went on.

"There'll be a war. Clumps of earth will rain down on coffins. Mothers will be left without sons, children without fathers, wives without husbands. Many will wake up without a roof overhead, and there will be blind men and cripples, and fear will choke off everything like a fog creeping over the valleys. Blood will flow down from the slopes and soak into the sand of the desert, and dry river beds will be filled with tears, and moans will resound throughout the land. But nothing will change, and the earth will keep on spinning round the sun, and the moon and stars will remain in their orbits just like after all the other wars, just as the smallest cog in the machine ruling the world hasn't budged a fraction of an inch. Not even when the tombs of the dead are piled up as high as the sky."

Only now did I understand that he wasn't talking to himself but to the One Who had created that world order, Who was responsible for setting the machine in motion so it would never stop, so that each cog would mesh with the others and everything would go on spinning at a fixed speed around the fixed orbit and nothing in the world would divert it without an order from on high.

"There'll be a war," I heard him repeat and I saw his eyes try to pierce the dark ceiling and see higher and wider. "There'll be a war just like then and, like then, You'll only look down on what's happening through a star-studded screen and You won't do anything, You won't even move a finger. Because You're just like Adam Wahn. Like the juggler Wahn—only worse!"

On that night and many other nights, Max Himmelfarb talked like that with the One Who had created the order of the universe and kept it going but Who seemed to consider it more important for the machine to keep turning than to make men stop killing each other and dam up the bloody stream that flowed through the splendor of the flowers on the slope.

"You're just like Adam Wahn. Worse, worse!" he repeated over and over, heaping up curses and complaints. The night was darker than a dense forest, and nothing came through the thickness.

I stayed on his windowsill until I saw that he had fallen asleep. As for me, I didn't sleep much that night. Unlike Max, I had never judged Adam Wahn harshly. First, because I believed that you can't judge anybody unless you stand in his shoes and, second, because I had not forgotten how much we had all wanted to stay alive. Almost everybody wanted to go on living; the ones who didn't simply died like flies.

Some never stopped repeating that only now did they know what they had really lost. And they didn't mean

Persian carpets and fur coats or the rungs of the ladder they'd hoped to climb in their careers, or the laurels they hadn't yet won—but the aroma of every rose they hadn't imbibed to the full, every rustle in the trees they hadn't listened to with awe. Now, they sighed, now, they had learned how to live.

Others didn't say why they wanted to stay alive. Maybe they had a strong survival instinct, or they were too cautious and clever to trust others with what they intended to do with their lives if they made it. Of all the thousands of camp inmates, I met only two who didn't conceal the fact that their thirst for life could be quenched only by revenge. There was a time when I thought Adam Wahn might be one of those.

On the other hand, there were a lot of people like me who wanted to survive most of all to bear witness. For years so much indescribable cruelty, so much inhuman horror, so much unimaginable evil, so much that was incredible had gone on around us—we were afraid that people could never believe it. We had to do everything to bring the truth to light. That was our only mission: to tell others, to bear witness. To accuse. I already knew I would never be a judge again, but I did want to be a witness and maybe because I had once been a judge, my testimony would be more credible.

To bear witness, to fight the battle against oblivion, that was our mission. We didn't think about punishment, an eye for an eye to the third or fourth generation. Nor did we care about sinning and forgiving. What court could pass judgment on the abysmal depths of all those crimes? What punishment could begin to be sufficient? And who could forgive or not forgive what was beyond all human understanding? What we did care about was not to let the world forget. To bear witness, that was our goal and, more than anything else, that was what kept us alive.

But none of us—not I nor anyone else—has ever given a complete account. The burden was so heavy that each of us could carry only a small seed and, even if we were infinitely persistent with it, like an army of ants, all we could pile up would be a little anthill at the foot of the huge mountain of all we couldn't carry on our backs and all we had lost along the way. And maybe also a mountain of all we had forgotten ourselves while we were fighting the battle against forgetting.

And whenever I thought about all the things covered by the thick snow of forgetting, I couldn't help thinking about Adam Wahn.

There were four of us. One, the poor dwarf with the ridiculous name of Leo Riesenberg, was crushed by death like a nut in the jaws of a nutcracker. Two, Max Himmelfarb and I, found one another again in Jerusalem but, although we saw each other every day, we almost never talked about those years in Major Kohl's court. And if one of us brought up a memory from that time, it was something we could laugh about and not one of the horrors. Max now told people about the ancient times, and I was still quarreling with God but couldn't talk to anybody about it because I didn't know what to say. It was the only legal case I still cared about, but most of the time I didn't know if I was playing judge or prosecutor. In any case, for years now the trial hadn't progressed by an inch.

That takes care of three of the quartet of court jesters of Camp Commandant Kohl. The last one, the juggler Adam Wahn, simply got lost. He disappeared after our trip out of hell and, ever since, Max and I hadn't come across the smallest trace of him. At first, we mentioned his name often, then only from time to time, until we finally gave up all hope of ever seeing him again. But even if we seldom talked about the juggler, that didn't mean that the riddle of his disappearance didn't stay with us. Nor did it mean we had completely lost all desire to solve it. It was like hoping to find one particular fish in the sea.

14

In those tense weeks before what would be called the Six Day War, Max Himmelfarb lived in a state of constant excitement. That worried me because, though his mind was lucid, I knew how much horror and pain he had to go through to get to that level of clarity. The fear that something would snap in that tortured brain never left me.

Things got even more serious after those six June days of glory when we were all drunk with victory. Max took to bringing the most bizarre stories to our nightly meetings at Menachem's kiosk. The stories themselves were wonderful, but they had the flavor of strong wine to be drunk carefully, in small sips.

I sensed a danger in these stories, not only because I

didn't know what to do with them but also because they didn't seem to be from this world. I couldn't escape the fear that Max's mind was moving on a very narrow bridge between the solid ground of reality and the turmoil of his dazed imagination. There was some quality in all those stories he brought to our corner, something that could shove him off that bridge and into the darkness.

One night, for example, he was terribly excited and told us he had met a man on Jaffa Road whom he hadn't seen in twenty years. I must admit that such a thing is unusual since, in Jerusalem, you don't have to look very long to find anyone. You just have to cross the triangle of Jaffa Road, King George, and Ben-Yehuda Streets a couple of times and if you don't see the person you're looking for, something's wrong. If you don't run into somebody for years, it means he's either died or left the country. Logically, then, if you do meet someone after many years, it means he's come back either from a long stay abroad, or from the dead. (That also happened once in Jerusalem, and Menachem Salz didn't think there was any need to get all excited about it.) But the man Max had met after so many years had his own story (as if, said Menachem, there's anybody in this city who *doesn't* have his own story).

Twenty years before he had been the caretaker of one of the many synagogues in the Old City. There were dozens of men like him in Jerusalem, and Max would probably never have known this one if the man hadn't disobeyed the Mandatory authorities. The British claimed that the Arabs were liable to interpret the Shofar blowing ceremony as a signal for a Jewish attack or use it as a pretext for an uprising of their own, and so blowing the Shofar on the Jewish Holy Days was forbidden. Every year that man came to the Western Wall and blew the Shofar on Yom Kippur. That was the man Max had met and whose story he now told us with such excitement.

In 1948, during the War of Independence, when the Jews were forced to flee from the hordes of rampaging Arabs and abandon their homes and shops in the Old City, the caretaker locked the door of the synagogue and all he took with him was the shofar wrapped in a prayer shawl and the big key he carried with him day and night, hung on a string around his neck. For twenty years he hadn't left his house in Mea Shearim except to go to the prayerhouse next door. Now, for the first time, he left and went back to the Old City with the key around his neck. Instead of the synagogue, he found only a pile of rubble. He had a key but there was no gate to unlock. Therefore, he decided that a gate had to be built with a lock to fit the key and that there was no time to lose.

On the day he met Max after so many years, the caretaker told him, joyously, that the gate was standing once again. He opened it with the big key he had worn around his neck for twenty years and locked it again since, for the time being, the gate didn't lead anywhere. Now he had a gate and a key. All he needed was a synagogue. "We'll build that too," he shouted at Max as they parted. "With God's help, we'll build it. We can still use some of the old stones."

"Think of it!" Max couldn't get over it. "Just think of it! A key without a gate! A gate without a building! Did you ever hear of such a thing? A key without a gate and a gate without a building!" He repeated it over and over while Menachem Salz only shrugged, and I thought more about the delicate balance of Max's mind than about the hidden meaning of his story.

Another night he came to the kiosk much later than usual, after all the pink nacre had already fallen to the horizon, and the sky was the color of a coxcomb, and the tea Menachem always made had grown cold. He told us what had delayed him. He couldn't tear himself away from a group of people gathered around two men arguing about whether we should make archeological digs to find out what's under the city, what's been buried there for hundreds of years, what we don't yet know and even what we do know, just to know for sure that everything is the way it's written.

"Down there, deep under the city, there's another city and, under that, another one and another one deeper down and that's where all our glory is," said one of them. "Without that, we're nothing. Just one more city, like all the rest."

"Glory?" his opponent objected. "What glory? Under other places there are also a lot of ancient cities. They fell one after another; one pile of debris is just like any other. Time buries all ruins, and new cities rise up everywhere on top of them. But only here over Jerusalem is there another Jerusalem in heaven hovering over us, and that's the only one that will never be burned down and that no cannons can destroy."

"Nonsense!" the other one swept all this aside. "What's underneath us and what's in front of us, that's what you can see. You can dig it up. You can touch the stairs Herod walked on. You can touch the stone table King David may have written on. But have you ever seen that Jerusalem hovering somewhere in the sky?"

"We're blind. That's why we can't see it. We're blind like newborn pups and our eyes are not open yet. But even blind puppies grope the way to their mother's milk. Otherwise they would die. And we can't live without the city above us either, that other Jerusalem in heaven. In the end, your eyes will be opened too and you'll see it. Then you'll know that our glory is over our heads and not under the stones we walk on."

They stood there in the street quarreling violently, and, as Max told us about the argument, his sympathies went back and forth between the sides until he finally asked us what we thought. Menachem Salz replied with a shrug, and as for me, as always, I preferred not to be a judge.

Max found more and more stories like that. There must have been thousands of them in the air, and he seemed to snatch them up and bring them to the kiosk as a bird catches flies and brings them to his nest one by one. After every story, Menachem would admit to me that he felt as if he had had one drink too many. I didn't admit that every one of the stories made me more and more afraid of what was going on in Max's mind and intensified my sense that the string was stretched too tight.

I was wrong. My fears were groundless; none of those stories caused a collapse and I was finally convinced that, even though Max Himmelfarb was easily excited, he was now a balanced individual, saner than all the rest of us. Indeed, because of one of Max's stories, it was I who lost my balance a few months later.

"You won't believe what happened to me today," he began even before we had time to say hello. Every word of his was accompanied by an excited gesture. "You won't believe it. I come with a group of American tourists to the Wailing Wall and give them the same spiel I always do. All of a sudden, as I'm pointing to the old destroyed Jewish Quarter, one of them comes up to me, a man in a loud checked shirt and a cap only jockeys wore in my day, with a necklace of cameras dangling from his neck, and he grabs my hand, looks at the number on my arm and says: 'That's really funny. Yesterday I met a man who had the next number.' That can't be, I tell him. 'Why not? I saw the same number myself with my own eyes except, at the end, where you have a six, he had a seven.' You're wrong, I tell him; I happen to know who has the number after mine and, if that man's still alive, God only knows where he is, but he sure isn't in Jerusalem. Then the man almost got mad at me. 'What do you mean?' he says. 'Benny Levy's never wrong. You can bet on that. Here'—and he points to his forehead— 'here they gave Benny Levy a computer.'

"Naturally I could only shrug. But to make sure, I asked him where he saw the man who had the number after mine, and when he said Mea Shearim I was sure, of course, that it was pure nonsense. That's the last place in the world Adam Wahn would live. But I admit that it really shook me up, and I still haven't gotten over it. Can you believe it?! For more than thirty years we've been looking for him and haven't found a trace of him, like he sank into the ground, and all of a sudden a complete stranger comes and tells you he saw him only yesterday, just a few feet away. I'm pretty much immune to surprises, but such a thing can throw even the calmest man off the track."

Max Himmelfarb got right back onto the track again. But I couldn't stop thinking about it. Of course, I had trouble imagining Adam Wahn living in the most orthodox religious section of Jerusalem, but God only knows what can happen to a man after thirty years, I said to myself, especially after what the juggler had gone through. Moreover, as my clairvoyance has grown weaker with age—and, in the case of Adam Wahn, I had lost it altogether—I've come to believe more and more in what people call coincidence. In short, I couldn't get it out of my system and so began stealthily to walk around Mea Shearim.

Although that section was built only about a hundred years ago, whenever I go there I feel like I'm walking around in the Middle Ages. The only people who live there are those who follow all six hundred and thirteen of God's commandments to the letter. They wear black caftans and fur-trimmed hats, just like their ancestors in the ghettos hundreds of years ago, and live their lives the same way too. My imagination wasn't strong enough to picture Adam Wahn living like that—and no one there could live any other way.

Nevertheless, for weeks, whenever I was in the area, I would walk around in that alien world whose mysterious atmosphere was somehow attractive. I got into conversations with men who looked like they came from another planet. I asked all of them about Adam Wahn, but no one knew him or had ever heard his name.

Later on, I found out that Max Himmelfarb had also devoted his free time during those days to the same search, in secret like me, but he hadn't had any success either. In the end, without either of us knowing what the other was doing, we both gave up at about the same time and reconciled ourselves to the idea that even Benny Levy's computer could sometimes be wrong.

But the mystery of the lost juggler kept bothering me. I knew what had happened to only three of Major Kohl's four court jesters. Something was missing. It was like listening to a symphony when all of a sudden the cellos or the trumpets or the flutes just drop out. All the time I was a judge, and afterward too, I always liked order. Maybe I've even been a bit pedantic about it. At the end of every trial, I liked to see the results of the investigation fitting all together like a nicely formed mosaic, with every stone in place. I didn't like fringes. All the strings had to be tied up together in the end and rolled into a ball, my sign for the end of a trial that brought the world back into balance. Like the billiard balls the juggler Wahn tossed up into the air, let circle in their orbit, and brought back to his hand. Impossible to imagine that one of them would deviate from its course and disappear into the mists of oblivion. I couldn't stop struggling against that.

And there was one more thing I couldn't forget. Everything we had salvaged from oblivion was here in this city, which was higher by one more layer of the dust of the six million. So I believed that if I could find out anything about the fate of Major Kohl's last jester, it would be here in Jerusalem.

We didn't go to Mea Shearim anymore, but ever since Max met Benny Levy, we talked about Adam Wahn a lot more.

"What if he walked by right now and stopped and asked the two of you how you were doing?" Menachem Salz suddenly asked us one night. "Would you be surprised?" Apparently he said that to fill a pause in our conversation, not because he expected an answer. But Max Himmelfarb never let a question go unanswered if he could help it.

"Not really," he said.

"What do you mean?" I had to demand an explanation.

And Max replied: "Here, in Jerusalem? Here anything can happen."

And I could only agree with him.

15

The very next day, Jerusalemites got a most violent reminder of the kind of things liable to happen here.

It was a Thursday, the day when everyone tries to buy what they need for the rest of the week because everything closes on Friday at noon and no one cooks on the Sabbath. Food must be prepared on Friday, and every good housewife tries to finish her shopping on Thursday. So that day the market at Machane Yehuda was full of customers, mostly women and old men doing the family shopping while the young people were still at work. People gathered around the stands, and traffic streamed up and down the narrow lanes of the market. They compared prices, tried to find the best fruit and vegetables, and haggled with the peddlers who bragged about their merchandise at the top of their lungs while keeping an eye on their scales. Everyone calculated how to buy the best goods at the lowest prices.

All this noisy bustle was suddenly drowned out by the crash of an explosion, and, after a split second of tense silence, came screams of panic, moaning, and weeping. Police, ambulances, and journalists reached the spot with admirable speed. Within a few minutes the radio was already broadcasting the news of the harvest of blood from the latest terrorist attack: three killed and fourteen wounded.

It wasn't the first time and no one thought it would be the last. We had gotten used to such things and had learned to live with them. As usual, the authorities would wait a few hours before they published the names of the wounded, and everyone was eager to make sure none of their relatives were among them. During those few hours life got back to normal. Motors and saws and drills started up again in their usual way and, right next to the stand decimated by the explosion, peddlers soon stood shouting out the prices of the goods they had brought at dawn, that day as every other day.

We were listening to the news in front of Menachem's kiosk when they announced the names of the three who were killed. We didn't know any of them. But the next morning, as I was coming out of my house, Max Himmelfarb appeared unexpectedly at the corner, waving a newspaper at me.

"Did you read it?" he shouted, all excited though he knew I had stopped reading newspapers altogether and listened to the news on the radio only once a day at Menachem's kiosk in the evening. Max, on the other hand, listened to the news every hour on the hour and read the newspaper from A to Z before he went to work in the morning. Now he showed me that, after they had published the names of those who were killed yesterday, the morning papers also printed a list of the wounded. And there he found the name he was running to show me. He stood still and pointed with his long bony finger to a line in the list:

Wahn, Adam, Mea Shearim.

"How about that?" he said. "So that American with the built-in computer was right after all. There couldn't be anyone else named Adam Wahn living in Mea Shearim with one number higher than mine on his arm, though we both thought that was the last place on earth we'd find him."

I had to admit that even coincidences had their limits. Anyway, we had no trouble confirming our assumption because the newspaper also listed what hospitals the wounded had been taken to.

Wahn? Adam Wahn? Yes, he's one of the severely wounded. Relatives? No? Then, unfortunately, they can't tell us any more. In any case, in the meantime, he can't see anyone.

While we were carrying on negotiations with the door-keeper and with the young nurse at the reception desk, whose well-developed bosom covered the list of wounded who had been admitted to the hospital, Max suddenly broke off in the middle of a sentence, grabbed my sleeve, and pointed with his sharp chin to a corner where a man in a caftan was facing the wall and praying with rhythmical motions.

"Remember?" Max asked me. "That's the man I met after

twenty years. You know—the key with no gate, the gate with no building. That's him. I'm sure they've already rebuilt at least half his synagogue by now."

"Didn't you tell me he hadn't left Mea Shearim for twenty years?"

"My God, of course! Why didn't I think of it before?"

We waited until the man loosened the belt of his caftan as a sign that he was finished praying—while praying, a pious man must separate the part that strives for heaven from the part he shares with the beasts—and, as soon as he sat down on the bench against the wall, we approached him.

"I'm sorry we meet here," Max greeted him. "Somebody in your family? Nothing serious, I hope."

No, no one in his family, but a good friend was wounded in yesterday's explosion. Really? We too—and here Max introduced me—came to ask about a friend whose name we found this morning in the list of wounded. I added that we were all together in a concentration camp during the war, that we had gone through a lot of horrors together so naturally we wanted to make sure our friend Wahn wasn't in any danger.

"Wahn? Wahn, you said?" asked the man in the caftan, surprised. "That's the friend I came to ask about. They won't tell me any more than what they probably told you. But they don't know me. I won't leave here till they let me see him."

We didn't have so much faith or persistence so we left after a while. Max asked the man from Mea Shearim to tell Wahn, if he saw him, that Max Himmelfarb and Judge Cahana had asked about him. We also agreed to meet again so he could tell us when we could visit Wahn.

There must be something to the notion that patience is the best soil for roses because the man who had worn the key of the destroyed synagogue around his neck for twenty years finally succeeded in this task as well. Max met him the next day and found out that, although it was impossible to talk with Wahn, who was unconscious most of the time, the man did see the doctor who was taking care of him. When the doctor heard that Wahn didn't have any family and that the man in the caftan was closer to him than anyone else in the world, he finally gave in and drew him a general picture of Wahn's condition.

Now we knew that the explosion had ripped off his right arm at the shoulder. There was still some hope of saving his right leg, which was also seriously wounded, but he would never use it again because his spine had also been damaged and the lower part of his body would almost certainly be paralyzed forever. So, unless complications appeared—and you could never rule that out—Wahn would survive once again, but would be crippled. It would be a few more days before he could have visitors.

That's what Max brought us. After thirty years of searching, we found Adam Wahn again just when he was condemned to be a poor cripple. A juggler without an arm. He'd never toss up those billiard balls and make them spin in their orbit. Of course, from the little bit of information Max had gleaned, Wahn had evidently given up juggling long ago and for the last three years had lived with Max's old friend. The man had given him a room in his apartment in Mea Shearim, but in fact he only slept there and spent most of his time studying in a nearby yeshiva. He earned his keep by cleaning the *mikveh* and heating the bath water. The *mikveh* was next door to the yeshiva and only two houses away from his room. So he spent his whole life in a space as big as a stone's throw. What had made Adam Wahn leave Mea Shearim and go to the market at Machane Yehuda on that ill-fated day remained a mystery, for the time being.

Less mysterious—for Max now solved this one—was where that American tourist had seen Adam Wahn. One of Wahn's jobs was to chop wood from time to time to heat the *mikveh* and to stack it neatly against the wall. This was done outside, and when he did it, he took off his coat and rolled up his sleeves. Benny Levy, the man with a computer in his head, was passing by at that very moment and his curiosity made him leave his group to go watch the man who was doing something unusual, and so he saw and recorded in his memory the number on the man's arm.

Nevertheless, there was still a great deal we wanted to know about Adam Wahn. What had he gone through, what had he done since we had traveled together out of hell? Where had he been for the last thirty years? What had brought him to Mea Shearim, of all places? But, most of all, questions I couldn't ask him then, years ago, but now I felt I could: What had bound him so strongly to life after he had lost everything? Why did he want so much to stay alive? Why was survival not just a desire but a command?

We had to wait until the doctors let Wahn have visitors, and all that time the juggler was always on our minds. Even though my belief in God had long since been poked as full of holes as an old sieve, it was still hard for me to believe that everything was meaningless. But what meaning could there be in Adam Wahn going through all he had just to survive, only to end up as a hopeless cripple? Every night before I fell asleep, I rolled the rock of that question up to the top of the mountain and each time found it down at the bottom, without an answer. A key with no gate, a gate with no building—it all got mixed up in my head and I tried in vain to convince myself that there was no connection between things. After all, you can put up a gate that will open again and be locked with a key, and you can erect a building where people can go in through the gate to pray. But no one could give Wahn back his wife shot by that criminal Walz right before his eyes, and no one could give him back his arm or his health destroyed by another criminal last Thursday at Machane Yehuda.

I couldn't wait for the moment when we would meet one another face to face again after so many years. I couldn't have said what was the real source of my curiosity, but I simply believed that seeing Adam Wahn would give me the answers to at least some of the many questions that kept coming back to plague me.

In a place so full of dreams as the street that leads to Jaffa Gate, people could dream of the strangest things. For a few nights I had dreamed the same dream. In it the juggler Adam Wahn comes to me and he still has two hands. Instead of colored billiard balls, he now tosses up heavy keys, catches them in flight, and throws them up again. Suddenly he stands in front of me without a right arm and all the keys fall down at my feet. I'm leaning against the post of the locked gate, but now I bend down to pick up the keys and I try them one by one. Only the last key turns in the lock and opens the gate, but behind the gate is an emptiness without any walls. Then, with his one hand, Wahn picks up a stone from the pile of rubble in front of the gate, brings it through the gate, and puts it on the ground where you can still see the traces of the destroyed building.

He brings another stone and then a third and begins to build a wall.

I didn't understand a thing about that dream. Night after night I woke up in the same place, and every time my impatience increased. It was hard for me to wait until I could see Wahn. Now I hoped to find the solution to my dream as well.

A week later Max finally told me we could visit Adam Wahn in the hospital the next afternoon. We spent a whole evening discussing what gift to bring him. This time even Menachem Salz didn't have any good advice. In the end we went empty-handed.

16

Next to a bed by the window sat the man from Mea Shearim, and he beckoned to us as we stood at the door. There was no mistaking the serious, long, drained face on the pillow, even if it was now framed by a dusty-gray beard and sweat-soaked sidelocks. It was the first time we had seen Adam Wahn with sidelocks. We recognized that narrow nose, the pointed chin, and the scar of his thin lips where words squeezed through, as through the crack of a slightly open door. And if we still doubted, we just had to look for a moment at those piercing black eyes, which even now, staring at the ceiling, had the same sparks and the same flame we remembered from the time in Major Kohl's court. The eyes that didn't turn away even for a split second from the colored billiard balls spinning in their orbit. Now, too, nothing escaped them.

He already knew about us so our visit didn't surprise him. The arch of his thin lips curved a bit more into a painful smile. We approached his bed almost on tiptoe, and he managed to get out a few words.

"What a way to meet again," he said. And after a long pause he added, "But it's good you came."

I touched the hand that had once saved his life with its skill and training. But then there had been another hand, just as nimble, and only the two of them together could work. Now the one hand that was left lay like an orphan on the blanket.

"You have to get well fast," I said, "so you can tell us about yourself. After so many years, you must have a lot to tell."

Quite often I catch myself with strange thoughts in my head, and I find it hard to talk about them with anybody. For instance, it grows dark and the night seems to don a judge's robes and stand in judgment on the day. Or I trip on a stone, and it occurs to me that Jerusalem is trying to tell me that things don't always go smoothly for her either, but it's always worth it to climb so high. Or I see a mountain on the horizon and say to myself: See, the earth has a hump too, even a thousand humps, and it still revolves with all its burdens. I'm so accustomed to these strange thoughts that what came into my head then didn't seem terribly odd.

Adam Wahn lay there with his eyes closed, and I saw that his eyelids were light blue. And I thought that two tears came down from heaven and fell on his eyes. But I didn't tell anybody.

"Yes, there's a lot to tell," Adam Wahn said at last in a

weak voice. "So many things I couldn't talk about before. Now I have to tell everything. It's good you came."

Even though I was terribly impatient, I told him he didn't have to hurry, that he had to get his strength back first and, if he wanted, Max and I would tell him about ourselves first. Of course, we were eager to hear about him, but we could restrain our curiosity for a while longer. Later, when he felt strong enough to tell us his tale, Max and I would take turns coming, and even then, I promised, we wouldn't tire him out.

We agreed to do that but it still took a long time until we could carry out our plan. Wahn complained of terrible pain in his amputated arm (which led to another of my strange ideas, that what's missing always hurts more than what we have). They had to give him painkillers that made him groggy. Whenever he was in such a state, we returned empty-handed from the hospital.

Even on days when he felt better, we were only allowed to stay for a half hour. One day Adam Wahn decided he felt strong enough and started to tell his story in a great rush, as if he wanted to make up for lost time and get to the point before it was too late. He spoke in short sentences, as if he were measuring with a precise ruler, and I couldn't tell if it was because he was short of breath or because he was now tossing up words as he had once thrown his colored billiard balls. He never once raised his voice.

"All the time I was there," he began, "I thought of only one thing: how to survive. Afterward, too, I thought of only one thing: how to get revenge. And even there I said to myself: Every one of us has to kill at least one of them. Later, after my wife's death, I promised myself to get mine. Every one would have his own man. Mine was Walz."

For a long time he was silent, staring at the white square of the ceiling. I could guess what was going through his mind as if a screen had come down and thousands of pictures were projected on it one after another, all rolled up on a reel. I was thinking I wouldn't hear any more that day when, all of a sudden, he began again.

"I had to find him. I didn't know where or how. Thousands of them disappeared. Go look for a needle in a haystack. They escaped. But I had to find him. Without rousing suspicion. They threw away their uniforms. Shaved their moustaches. Every one of them had a hiding place. They all knew where to wait out the hard times. Until the world forgot.

"I had no idea where Walz lived. I wound up in the American zone. There were dozens of DP camps. I landed in one of them. I wanted to get a little strength. Instead I got sick. For two months I was in the hospital. Only later did they tell me I'd had one foot in the grave already. Typhus. High fever all the time. I fantasized. They tell me I kept shouting: 'Walz, Walz, I'll find you. I'll kill you like a mad dog.' A young American doctor took care of me. He told me all that. A Jew from Germany in an American uniform. His family got out in time. He finished studying in America just before the war. He was like a brother to me. But he wanted to know about Walz. Finally I told him everything. He promised to help me find him."

Wahn didn't speak as clearly as this. Often he would break off the flow of his words and make a long pause between sentences and, during that break, he seemed to be wandering somewhere in the distance in his mind. Every time he came back to me, he would try to catch up by telling his story faster.

"He did help," he went on, "more than I could've hoped for. One day he came in very excited. He had been talking with a friend of his, another Jewish officer assigned to interrogate Nazi prisoners. They found a list of about 15,000 SS men. Walz's name appeared only once. Walz, Heinrich. He gave me a paper with Walz's personal details. Date of birth, date of enlistment in the SS. Above all, where he was living when he joined. A small town near Munich. Dr. Klein, my doctor, even found that out for me. I wanted to leave right away. No one in the whole world could be as strong as I felt."

The piece of paper worked like a wonder drug and Klein couldn't understand how Wahn suddenly began to recover so fast. A week later it was impossible to restrain him. He already saw himself on the way to the little town near Munich.

"Naturally, Klein tried to talk me out of it. Warned me of complications. Threatened to tie me to the bed. But when he saw it was hopeless, he gave me everything I needed. He even stuck a few dollars in my pocket, a couple cartons of cigarettes, and three pairs of nylon stockings. You could buy anything with that. Anything and anybody.

"The first thing I bought when I left the DP camp was a pistol. Like the ones the SS used. It wasn't hard to find. Ammunition wasn't a problem either. Other survivors just lay around on their cots in the camp. Didn't know what to do with themselves. Many still hoped to find some relatives. Still believed in miracles. Had nowhere to go. No one to come back to. For me it was different. I knew why I wanted to live. At least until I found Walz. Until I took revenge. I didn't think any further than that.

"I spent two days and two nights in a crowded train. I

didn't let go of my bag for a moment. Everything I owned was in it. Two shirts, trousers, two pairs of socks, a box of colored billiard balls, a deck of cards and a few other things I needed for my juggling. Even in the worst times, I knew I could make a living out of my pack. And, at the bottom were the pistol and the bullets. I didn't need anything else. I got to Munich on the third day. The train to Walz's town didn't leave for another hour. I sat in the smoke-filled waiting room thinking, for the first time, about what I was going to do next."

Wahn was out of breath and had to stop again for a while. In my mind, I sat on the bench with him in the waiting room, thinking of what I would have done in his place. Soon he felt strong enough to go on with his story.

"Even when I was sitting in the train, I wasn't much smarter. If I asked people, I'd rouse suspicion. But I couldn't leave anything to chance. I couldn't just walk around in the little town and count on running into Walz somewhere. What if he was hiding? He'd probably try to get back home as soon as possible. But maybe he'd think that was danger-ous. What if he was hiding somewhere else? The train went through a valley. On both sides of the track were mountains covered with thick forests. There must have been thousands of hiding places there that nobody could get to. Or the Americans might have arrested him already and he might now be in their camp. That was possible. I should have found that out before I set out head over heels, without thinking anything through. But I'd been traveling for three days. Was almost in the town. Going back was out of the question.

"Next to me was an elderly couple. He had obviously retired a long time ago. Maybe he'd been a railroad worker.

He was puffing on a carved little pipe with a metal cover. He kept nodding all the time and sometimes said things like, 'That's it,' or, 'We've come a long way.' She was very talkative. She chattered all the time and didn't mind that she was the only one interested in the conversation.

"I asked how many stops before we'd get to the town I was going to. The old man took the pipe out of his toothless mouth and said with absolute certainty that there were four. Then he added the exact minute the train was scheduled to arrive. The woman saw that as an opening for a broader stream of conversation. She didn't pass up the chance. I could get off the train with them, she said. They were going to the same place. In fact they lived in a village an hour's walk from there. They knew everybody in that town. And she assaulted me with a hundred questions. Who was I going to see? Where did I come from? I spoke very good German but naturally had trouble with the Bavarian dialect. Clearly, I wasn't from the town. I lied and said I was from the Sudentenland but had lived in Brno for several years. Who was I visiting? the old woman asked again. Huber. There were so many Hubers in the area I was sure there'd be one there. Huber? Which one? The innkeeper or the builder? The builder, I said. We were planning to do something together.

"Suddenly it occurred to me to add that I was also planning to visit a certain Walz. We were together during the war and I remembered that he was from here. Walz? That must be Heinrich, she said. That's it, Heinrich, I confirmed. Yes, she thought a few moments. She knew he'd come home not long ago. But, if she wasn't mistaken—and she usually wasn't because, under this kerchief, all is well— he had only warmed himself up a bit and disappeared right away. Just like that? Too bad, I said. Too bad? She didn't seem to agree. He was always a good-for-nothing. I could take it from her. People were saying it wasn't safe enough for him here. He was afraid. God only knows what he had on his conscience. Heinrich Walz had never been a good man. I pretended to be amazed by what she said. Maybe she knew where he might have gone? I asked innocently. People don't know anything for sure these days, she answered. They say he might have gone to Austria. Maybe the ground isn't so hot there. The old man puffed on his pipe, took it out of his mouth, nodded and said, 'We've come a long way.'"

Wahn looked at the clock on the wall and saw that visiting hours were almost over. He stopped only for a minute to catch his breath and then went on quickly.

"That was a blow. The woman sounded reliable. If she was right, my whole trip was for nothing. I didn't let her see my disappointment. We got off the train and I went part of the way with them. The old woman kept chattering all the time. I didn't pay any attention. The fact that I'd probably missed Walz threw me off balance. I didn't know then that I had a long way to go and that Walz would slip out of my hands many times. At the crossroads, the woman showed me where to find the builder Huber. And if I went down this road a little bit further, to the end of the town and then a bit more toward the forest, I'd come to the Walz farm. Then we parted.

"I had to make up my mind. I could take the woman's word for it, turn around, and take the next train back to where I came from. But maybe I should try to find out if the woman really wasn't mistaken. Finally I decided to take the road she'd shown me. I soon came to the farm that, according to her, belonged to the Walz family.

"The big wooden house indicated a solid farmer and not a poor peasant. It stood a bit apart, separated from other houses on one side by a strip of fields and on the other by the forest. I walked around the stables and the granary. Not along the front of the house where they could look out the windows and see the road. I didn't think Walz was still there. But I had to be careful. When I saw them airing out the haystack, I knew what I had to do. I went through two fields to the forest. Sat down on a clump of moss near the edge of the woods. From there I had a good view of the farm. I was hidden behind a high growth of ferns. I still had a little bit of food in my bag. I ate it and stretched out on the moss. When I woke up, it was late afternoon. But I still had to wait. I needed darkness to carry out my plan."

He looked again at the clock on the wall and speeded up his narrative as if he wanted at least to finish this part of his story in time, before I had to go.

"The first flames rose from the haystack and reached the granary in a minute. By that time, I was no longer in the forest. I was pressed flat against the ground in a ditch dividing the two fields. People ran out of the house, shouting. Ran back and forth, led the cattle out of the barn and passed buckets of water. I watched carefully. None of them could be Walz. I saw townspeople come running and trying in vain to put out the fire. The summer had been dry and, before the fire brigade got there, everything went up in a pillar of flame.

"I made a wide circle around the town. Waited for dawn and went back to the railroad station. This time, I didn't have to wait long for the first train. Three days later I was back in the DP camp. I had turned the Walz farm into a pile of ashes. But I considered that only a very small payment for an infinite debt. Now I was sure I had to look for him somewhere else. I knew that now. But nothing else."

At that moment the head nurse came in and announced in a shrill voice that visiting hours were over. Wahn moved as if to throw up his hands in resignation. It seemed as if he realized now for the first time that this was one of the many movements he would never make again because it couldn't be done with only one hand. He smiled. It was the first time I had ever seen anything like a smile on his face. He hurried to get to the end of the story.

"Naturally I looked for Klein right away. I didn't find him. They told me he'd been transferred to another camp. So I had to find another way to find out if Walz wasn't already behind bars. And if it turned out that they hadn't caught him, I had to find help and get papers so I could move around freely. If he really was in Austria, I had to go after him. But I see the nurse frowning already. So I'll tell you the end of it tomorrow."

I touched his remaining hand in farewell.

17

He told the next part of the story not to me but to Max, who took my place the next day and who told me the whole thing that night when we met at Menachem's kiosk.

As Max described it, Wahn unrolled the skein of his memory very slowly that day, lingering over every detail as if they were knots that had to be untied before he could go on unraveling the thread.

In the DP camp, Wahn told Max, you could find anything, get any information, buy any item. You simply had to seek patiently and never give up because you often went down a dead end and had to go back again until you finally found what you were looking for. There was a lively trade in information, and you just had to know whom to ask and how to pay for it.

Knot after knot, Adam Wahn untied all he still remembered about what he had gone through to make sure the Americans hadn't beat him to it and arrested Walz before he himself could put his hands around the man's neck. It wasn't easy to get the list of imprisoned SS men, and the names on it didn't mean much since they all had time to change their names and get hold of false papers.

At every step he came up against a wall of hopelessness. Logic demanded he give it up. At most, he could hope for a lucky break that might some day put Walz in his hands. But Wahn hated nothing more than abandoning himself to luck. So he let himself be guided by his feelings and not by his skeptical, doubting, and therefore useless mind.

In the information market of the camps there was a flood of rumors about SS men. The Nazis were mostly fleeing to Austria. According to these sources, a lot of them stayed there because it was easier to hide from the Americans in Austria than in Germany. Others, they said, escaped through Italy to more distant places, mostly to South America. The rumors told of an airtight network to help those war criminals escape from one place to another and of a ship that took them where they would never be found. It all seemed prepared with Prussian thoroughness. They knew that dozens, even hundreds, of murderers were fleeing the reach of justice every single day while no one seemed to be able to do anything about it. The Americans had their hands full with the ones already behind bars, and many of them also succeeded in clearing out.

Wahn's senses told him that if Walz hadn't stayed home—and for the moment, that was the only thing he was sure of—he probably wasn't anywhere else in Germany either. Admittedly, you shouldn't rely only on your senses; but reason, preaching futility, wasn't any good either. People who were helpless themselves were willing to help anyone who could make up his mind, even if the decision seemed absolutely foolish and almost no one believed in the success of his plan. So without too much trouble, Wahn finally managed to get a document that allowed him free passage over the border to Austria.

Wahn told Max how, in Austria, he had wandered from one camp to another, sent from Pontius to Pilatus, how everyone had heard a different rumor, everyone gave different advice, and how, at night, he was never any wiser than he had been at dawn.

He set off from Vienna to Innsbruck because the last rumors said that was the first stop on the flight over the Brenner Pass to Italy. On the way he stopped in Salzburg because other sources—and no one could confirm or deny their reliability with any more certainty than the other ones—said that the mountains in that region were swarming with hundreds of SS men. They were changing their uniforms for lederhosen and loden coats with bone buttons, and there they found a secure haven.

In Salzburg he met a man who had survived a half-dozen concentration camps and had worked with the Americans after the war interrogating prisoners and searching for escaped war criminals in hiding. But he had finally left them because he decided he could bring more criminals to justice more quickly on his own. He began collecting testimony about the horrors, documents about the criminals, and information about their activities and movements since the end of the war. He proposed that Wahn work with him.

When they first met, he discovered they had something in common. But, although he didn't talk about it, Wahn knew there was also something that drove them apart. One wanted legal punishment, the other revenge. Nevertheless, Wahn accepted the proposal and stayed in Salzburg a few months. Mostly because he hoped that working with his new friend might lead him to Walz's trail. Everything that helped the other man catch and punish criminals was certainly good and worthwhile. But everyone was mostly concerned with finding his own beast. His man was Walz, and he wanted to settle accounts with him himself. That was the only thing he had to accomplish.

Suddenly the two men got into an argument.

"Law," said Wahn's new friend. "Every one of them must be brought to trial. Every one of them must look witnesses in the eye. Every one who is proved to be a criminal must be punished. Every one must finally know that there is a law and that there is justice."

Wahn retorted with an onslaught of questions. "Law? And who are the judges? Who guarantees me that they themselves shouldn't be sitting where the accused are? Where do you find the jury? How do you know for sure that none of them had a brother, a friend who was no better than the one they have to judge? And what if they sentence him only to a couple of months or even let him go free?"

"Law! Above all, law must rule the world."

"Good," Wahn agreed. "Law should rule. But not the law everyone can bend to his need like a rod. Not a law that says others can judge things we've experienced, others who've never known such things. The punishment they inflict can never be enough."

"You talk like a child treated unfairly. What does sufficient punishment mean? What punishment can be enough for a tiny fraction of the horrors? Some of them killed dozens, maybe hundreds of helpless and innocent people with their own hands. You want to execute them a hundred times over?"

"My wife's murderer must not stay alive," Wahn insisted. "He won't stay alive. He won't get away with it. I've promised myself. And I don't rely on anybody in the world except myself. Here, with these two hands, I'll see to it that he doesn't stay alive."

"And then others will look for you just as you're looking for him now."

"No. They won't have to look for me. Because I'll have nothing more to do in the world. I have only one purpose and I'll carry it out."

That's how their quarrel ended every time, and that was how Max finished his story that night at Menachem's kiosk.

"Everybody's just different," noted Menachem as he filled an ice cream cone for a young customer. "Everybody's got a different flavor, everybody's got to be opened with a different key. Love sets one guy in motion, somebody else starts running when he sees a penny in the distance, and the only thing that drove Wahn was that he wanted revenge. Maybe he really had to. God only knows. This one's hounded by a heavy conscience, that one by some imbalance. Maybe he really had to. Maybe he really couldn't do it any other way."

"The law is the Ten Commandments," spoke the judge in me. "An eye for an eye, a tooth for a tooth was never the law."

"But Wahn knew only one law, the one he had given himself: My wife's murderer must not stay alive. That was all he had to live for." That was how Max saw the issue.

"That's just what I say. Everybody's different," Menachem Salz summed up our conversation.

Eventually Max resumed his tale about Adam Wahn's path to revenge.

A couple of months later, after his new friend had failed to convince him that his plan was insane and that he didn't have any chance of ever finding his man, Wahn left Salzburg for Innsbruck, as he had intended from the start. He didn't stay there very long either. He had gotten a passport in Salzburg and managed to find someone in Innsbruck who got hold of an Italian visa for him. He crossed the Brenner Pass in a truck and then wound his way slowly down to Genoa. Here and there someone helped him with a bed for the night, a piece of cheese, or a jug of wine. Sometimes, he would put his pack down next to the fountain in the middle of a town square, take out his colored billiard balls and throw them up in the air, one after another, spinning them in their orbit; the enchanted spectators who gathered around would drop a few coins in his hat on the sidewalk. So he always had enough to keep going on his way, to the port where he knew the ships sailed for South America.

Soon after he came to Genoa, however, he fell ill again. Either he had left the hospital in the DP camp too soon, or his weakened body couldn't stand the hardships of that eternal traveling. In any case, a strong attack of dysentery finally led him to the gate of the monastery hospital where the monks found him and had to take him in. They found a little money on him as well as some personal documents indicating that he had been a Jewish prisoner in a concentration camp in Germany, so they were certain that some Jewish organization would pay for him. They didn't know what to make of the colored billiard balls they found in the pack, but they didn't find the pistol or bullets for Wahn had buried them in the nearby park as soon as he felt the weakness coming on.

This time there was no one like the young Jewish doctor in the American camp, but if they didn't treat him like a brother, at least they did take good care of him. He had no reason to complain and, even if he had, it would have been difficult because they didn't want to speak German there, not even those who could speak it well, and Wahn's Italian was limited to a few dozen words. So, he would just lie quietly, let them take care of him, get better slowly, and think. His longing for revenge didn't grow weaker for a moment. The peace and quiet in which he could now think made him realize more clearly how hopeless his efforts were.

How could he hope even for a moment to find the man he was looking for? Go look for one specific teardrop in the sea. Go find one particular grain of sand in the desert. Every one is just like all the others and you can't know where the wind will blow it, where it will roll. Walz might have been hiding anywhere in the world at that moment. He could just as well have been here in Genoa, lying in the next bed, as at the other end of the world. Wahn lay all day, staring at the emptiness of the ceiling and seeing ever more clearly the hopelessness of his mission. He saw a whole life of searching ahead of him and, as he now understood ever more clearly, he would never reach his goal. Wasn't that ultimately the fate of every man? Didn't everyone seek, didn't everyone have to seek all his life and, in the end, only a few lucky people find what they're looking for?

If Adam Wahn had believed in God then, he would have told himself that only He could show him the trail. He would have told himself that he could end his travels right then and there or go back to the Bavarian town where Walz's family lived or begin all over again where he had lived with Esther before the war. If God wanted to give him a sign, He could do it anywhere. And if He didn't, there was no point in searching.

If he had believed in God. But at that time, and for long after, Adam Wahn was far away from the last trace of the belief he had lost. Yet, although he was convinced he had almost no chance of success, he was still obsessed with only one thing and couldn't give up the pursuit.

Logic told him that, even if an army went searching through the world for him, Walz might still find some refuge and escape. But Adam Wahn had long since stopped relying on anything in the world, including logic and intelligence. He believed only in himself. He had to concentrate everything in himself, his mind and his senses, like a magnetic needle that, he believed, would show him the way to Walz. In vain did logic warn him, and in vain did the clock on the wall laugh at him and call him a fool with its slow pendulum. Adam Wahn was waiting only for the moment when the door of the hospital would open and he could resume his search.

When that moment finally came, he was so weak he was forced to postpone his travels for a while. If he needed one more straw to break the back of his resistance to this wise decision, he didn't have to look hard for it. As soon as he left the hospital, he headed for the park where he had hidden his gun. All he found was an empty hole. Whoever had dug the hole and taken out the gun hadn't even bothered to cover it up again. Wahn knew that the first thing he had to do was get another.

Perhaps he could have gotten a little help during those hard times from the sources that had paid his hospital bill, but something inside him refused to accept it. Maybe he didn't want to be obligated to anyone else, and maybe he really didn't believe in anything but himself. And maybe that magnetic needle of his pointed in another direction. He left for the port but knew that, even if a suitable ship were at anchor there and even if the captain were willing to accept him as a stoker for the voyage to South America, in his present condition, he couldn't begin to think of hard work. He had to find another solution to get through the time he needed to recover. Dragging through the streets to the port, he suddenly stopped in front of a wooden fence covered with gaily colored posters.

One poster announced the appearance of the Prato Circus in Genoa, a middle-sized circus of sixteen horses, six lions, and three bears. He could see right away that it was splendidly managed. From the gate, Wahn was escorted by a uniformed circus employee past a spacious, clean tent to a group of gleaming, spotless circus cars. In front of one of those houses on wheels, which reminded Wahn—God knows why—of the story of Hansel and Gretel and their gingerbread house, a dwarf was exercising. Though his face proved that he was no youngster, he turned very nimble somersaults and cartwheels.

"You take him," the uniformed man said. "I've got to get back to the gate. He's looking for work; maybe the Signora will want to see him."

The little man stopped his exercises and bowed politely.

"My pleasure," he said. "I'm always happy to go to the Signora. What language does he speak?" he asked, and the man in the circus uniform replied that Wahn spoke Polish and German along with a little French and understood some Italian.

"*Po polsku? Prosze pana,*" said the dwarf, but before taking Wahn to the Signora, he squatted down again and looked at the stranger as if he were measuring the height of a church tower. Then he jumped up, glanced at Wahn's hands and said: "A juggler, balls, bottles, rings, plates, cards. You're in luck. A Chinese fellow just left us three days ago, and we just happen to have a little hole in our program."

Wahn was led to Signora Prato, who was sitting at a desk in one of the circus cars. Even as she sat there, he could easily imagine her balancing on a horse. Although no longer young, she was one of those women whose beauty never fades. Her soft, brown eyes were piercing, as if she were looking deep inside him. She peered at Wahn's face for a long time as if trying to read who he was, what had happened to him, what experiences he had gone through — this man standing in front of her asking for work. She told him in French not much better than his own that, as little Ricardo had certainly already told him, they were indeed looking for a juggler just then. She asked if he had recommendations, wanted to know his past experience. She spoke slowly and kept staring at him, probing Wahn's sad face as if she were fascinated by it.

Wahn said he had never needed written recommendations because those who saw him work didn't ask for them. He didn't need anything, in fact, but a little more space and, if she wanted to see a sample of his work, with her permission, he would show her something even here—or, as he preferred, on the lawn outside. Without waiting for her permission, he took off his coat and rolled up his sleeves. As he bent over to take the billiard balls out of his pack, his eyes touched her face and he saw that all the blood had drained out of it. Her lips trembled and her fear-filled eyes were fixed on his arm with the concentration camp number tattooed on it.

"It was like a serial novel," Max concluded his daily report. "As soon as tension begins to build up, the head nurse comes in and there's no haggling with her. I had to say good-bye and leave."

*18

I didn't like Adam Wahn very much the next day. His fever had gone up a bit, he complained of pains in the hand he no longer had, he spoke more excitedly than before, as if he felt driven to tell me as much as possible. So he soon ran out of breath. A few times I offered to sit next to him quietly for a while and come back later for the rest of the story. But Wahn insisted on continuing. First he made sure that Max had in fact told me everything he had heard the day before. I assured him that Max had brought the story up to the amazement on Signora Prato's face when she saw the number tattooed on his arm. Like an actor waiting for his cue, he went on precisely from that point, right where he had stopped the day before.

"Amazement?" he said. "Maybe it was amazement, or panic, or maybe something else. She seemed paralyzed. For a while I didn't know what happened. Then she regained her speech. Her husband, Giacomo Prato, it turned out, had been one of the few thousand Italian Jews transferred by the Germans to Auschwitz and killed as soon as they got there. Maybe they also tattooed numbers on their arms before they sent them to the gas chambers—for the sake of order. I don't know. Anyway, Signora Prato had certainly heard about it. Now, for the first time in her life, she saw such a number with her own eyes.

"'Everyone has his own story,' she said at last. 'One day you'll tell me yours. You don't have to show me anything now. You're hired. Ricardo will show you where you'll live and explain everything. Come to the show tonight. You can start working tomorrow. If you need anything, come straight to me.'

"As I rolled down my sleeves, she looked at my arm again with that same abysmal sadness. I could imagine what was going on inside her right then. But something was going on inside me too, and I understood that even less. Not what you think. She was still a beautiful woman, but for me Esther was the last. I didn't, couldn't touch another woman after her. That was another reason I had to kill Walz."

Then, although talking was clearly hard for him that day, Wahn told me what had really happened to him at that moment. For the first time he seemed to be moved like a chess piece on a big board, advancing and retreating with other pieces, in moves that were incomparably more complicated than those of the knights, bishops, and rooks in a real game. All he knew was that, in the end, he would have to checkmate the black king, but he didn't see him on the board at all and didn't know where to find him in the multitudes of squares. But whoever was moving the pieces did know. For the first time, the consciousness burst in him that someone seemed to be moving him in the right direction. If not, how could he explain all the stations along his way, which would certainly be even longer? Doctor Klein, the chatting woman in the train to Walz's hometown, the man in Innsbruck who knew everything about the escape routes of the SS men, Signora Prato and the dozens of others who had helped him get papers and everything else he needed. Each of them alone might have been a coincidence; all of them together formed a chain he could hold as he climbed and new links were constantly added to it.

And that very night, after the show, the chain would grow by one more link.

"Ricardo was waiting for me in front of Signora Prato's trailer," Wahn went on. "When I told him I was hired, he turned a big cartwheel for joy. I don't know why but he liked me at first sight, and now there was nothing he wouldn't do to help. Before he introduced me to the manager, he took my pack and said: 'We'll go by my place and you can leave this there for the time being. Besides, I've got an idea. God knows where they'll put you. What about staying with me? We'll be there in a minute. It's not bad. For one dwarf, it's really too big. There's enough room for both of us. I don't snore and I don't bring girls home. If you agree, I'd regard it as a great honor.' Once again he bowed low to me as a Spanish grandee and began to shake his big head on his little torso. His mouth, wrinkled like a crab-apple, opened in a broad grin: 'What do you say?'"

Wahn had no reason to say no, and from that day on he

shared a trailer with Ricardo. Everything was neat and cozy, and he felt better there than anywhere else since the war. Little Ricardo was a wonderful man. Sometimes, in his desire to cheer Wahn up, he would behave like a mischievous child; sometimes he was wiser than anyone Wahn had ever known. He had a full store of jokes but also knew when to keep quiet. He never asked any questions, and when—perhaps just because of that—Wahn began to talk, Ricardo knew how to listen better than anyone else. Adam Wahn had never made friends so fast with anyone before.

At night, after the show, they would sit up until after midnight, talking about themselves. Wahn discovered a lot about the world of dwarfs from Ricardo and told him about those things that never left him for a moment. About crimes that had to be judged and, if God didn't punish the guilty, every man had to do it himself so that the sinners didn't go free.

For a long time, Wahn spoke in a general way about what he had seen in the camps and not about what he had gone through himself. He kept warning himself to be careful and not say too much. But one evening, he could no longer contain himself and told Ricardo about our lives in Major Kohl's court. Even now, he didn't tell about his wife's death or about Walz. He told Ricardo only about the four of us and when he came to Leo Riesenberg, Ricardo suddenly jumped up and cried out excitedly: "Leo! My long lost friend! Where is he? Where is he?"

"Maybe I should've kept quiet," Adam Wahn was sorry even now, years later. "But I didn't understand until too late."

When he heard how Leo had died, little Ricardo crept

into a corner and began to weep like a child. It took him a long time to calm down. Then he told Wahn the story. He had known Riesenberg well. There were three of them: the trio of dwarfs, the best in the world. Himself, Leo, and Charles Duval, who was known in France as Charlemagne. In the Circus Hagenback, they were called the Three Musketeers. They'd fence with tiny cardboard swords and the people laughed themselves sick. Then Leo wasn't allowed to perform in Germany, and the others also decided to leave because of that. Ricardo came back home to Italy and Duval left Europe altogether. For some time he performed in America, where they called him Charlie the Sheriff because no one knew what Charlemagne meant. Later he married a female dwarf from Argentina and settled in Buenos Aires. His wife came from a wealthy family and Duval had a little money himself, so he retired from the circus and began to paint. Though first it was nothing but a hobby, in recent years he had had several successful exhibitions, sold pictures in America, and seemed to be making a good living. They still kept in touch with Ricardo and corresponded a few times a year. Now Ricardo would have to tell him the sad news that only two of the Three Musketeers were left. Poor Leo, poor little thing.

"All of a sudden, I felt again like someone was reaching out to me," Adam Wahn continued. "I didn't know a living soul in all of South America. I only knew that I had to get there at any cost because I believed—maybe without any logical reason—I just believed I could find Walz there. It hit me like a bolt of lightning that Leo's friend was destined to help me. Suddenly I was sure that Charles Duval, the French dwarf swept off to Buenos Aires and coincidentally the friend of the two other dwarfs I had met in my life, was my next link. Maybe this was the last favor of friendship that Leo Riesenberg did for me.

"I asked Ricardo to mention me in his next letter to Duval and to add that I planned to come to South America. I didn't yet know when I'd make it, but I hoped to get there in the not too distant future. With his permission, I'd get in touch with him as soon as I reached Buenos Aires and tell him more about our mutual friend. I didn't know why but, right then, I felt I was closer to my goal. It took another year till I saw how precise the magnetic needle was in the compass of my senses."

Now Wahn accelerated the pace of his story, skipped a whole year and got to Buenos Aires as if he were changing slides in a projector. I didn't feel that he was bored with telling his story but that he was racing through it like someone who doesn't have much time. As if he had read my mind, he tried to divert me from my thoughts rather than talk me out of them.

"Everything that happened during that year until I rang the bell of the little villa in Buenos Aires where Charles Duval and his wife lived just wasn't important," he said. "It wasn't a bad year. I felt at home in the Prato Circus. Ricardo was a fine friend, conditions were good, and Signora Prato treated me well."

He seemed to consider for a while if that was enough and then added: "We became friends. The number on my arm helped." Suddenly I realized that, along with his arm, Wahn had also lost his number.

"I had to tell her everything about me," he went on, "and everything we'd gone through. She was the only one I trusted. I didn't even tell Ricardo everything. She was the only one who knew that nothing else in my life had any meaning. Just to find Walz and take revenge. She often tried to talk me out of it. Finally, I had to promise her that, if and when I did find Walz, I'd leave his punishment to the courts and be satisfied to be the accuser and not the hangman. In return, she agreed to help me get to Buenos Aires or any other place in South America. I think she knew I couldn't keep my promise but she helped me anyway. She had friends and relatives among the shipowners and seamen in Genoa, and one of them, the captain of a freighter about to sail for South America, took me on. They gave me easy work, and at night I had to teach the captain a few card tricks. But none of that's important," he hurried on.

The only important thing was that he had finally reached the place where he hoped—no, where he strongly believed—he was closer to his goal. And the goal of his long trip was also the only one he still lived for.

He was no longer surprised that he immediately found friends behind the door of the little white house, in a well-tended garden. He had to love the Duvals at first sight. They reminded him so much of the good dwarfs in Mother's long-forgotten fairytales. Now he was sure that people were unwittingly sending him from station to station on a clearly marked road and every one of them knew only the next section and nothing else. Sometimes he felt like a brick passed from hand to hand to its proper place in the high wall of the building. Now he moved with the certainty of a sleepwalker, putting one foot in front of the other on a tightrope, and step after step brought him closer to his goal. He felt himself changing: from an object passed on by others, he came back to being someone who wasn't sent but who sent himself; from the heavy clay that bricks are made of, he became the master builder who knows just where to put the last brick, to press it and set it in place so it won't move anymore.

Charlie Duval's childish little hands were not big enough to cover his oversize face. He also needed the soft hands of his little wife in which to bury his head when he heard what Wahn told him about their mutual friend. For a long time they stood silently, as if they were standing over the grave of Leo Riesenberg, the Jewish dwarf who wanted to unite all the dwarfs of the world. It was only after a while that Duval, his face livid with hatred and rage, spat out two unexpected words: *"Sales vaches."* Adam Wahn wasn't old enough to remember that this expression of fury and contempt was born in the First World War, but he did know what the words meant and saw them as two lights at the end of a dark tunnel. Signals. No more doubt. He and Duval spoke a common language.

Charles Duval could hardly have said why he reached out to Adam Wahn across the table. Evidently he felt a need for more confirmation. For Wahn, it was like a seal on a treaty even if, for the time being, only one of them knew what was written in it.

*˙*19

For three weeks we came to the hospital every day, I one day and Max the next, and at night, at Menachem's kiosk, we carefully pieced together all the shards of Adam Wahn's feverishly told story we had learned that day. Once or twice he hadn't slept the night before and was too weak to talk, and then we could only say hello and promise to come back the next day. But most of the time he didn't show any signs of weakness; he seemed to be waiting for our visits and insisted on telling his story to the end. As if driven by some impulse, he managed to cram months and often years of the past into the half-hour we were allowed to stay with him.

It was a long time after he met the Duvals that he finally told them about himself. Ultimately, he even told them how his wife had been killed. Then he casually mentioned that the man who killed her had disappeared from Germany like so many others. He didn't hide his suspicion that the man was hiding, surely under an assumed name, in this part of the world and, who knows, maybe even in Buenos Aires. Charles Duval said only: "*Sales vaches.*" Months went by before they returned to the subject.

In the meantime, Wahn worked making automobile batteries in a small factory owned by one of Mme. Duval's brothers. All her brothers were handsome and well-built; she was the only one who had stopped growing as a child, and her brothers would have given her the moon if she had wanted it. Wahn rented a room from an old widow whose husband had been a supervisor in the factory and whose life had been cut short by a street brawl between political factions, the sort of fight that was fairly common in that country. Wahn could certainly have performed as a juggler in one of the many nightclubs downtown and would have made two or three times as much money as he brought home every weekend from the factory; but, first of all, he didn't need any more and, most important, he warned himself not to appear in any place where there was the slightest danger of being recognized. He had to surprise the man he was looking for and not be surprised by him. Spending eight hours a day in the factory where almost no one spoke any other language helped him learn Spanish fast. The work itself wasn't hard and, because he was concentrating on his goal, his time passed in thoughts that were not only about what his hands were ordered to do.

For months, patiently and unobtrusively, he collected everything he could find out about the Germans in Argentina, organized his data on the basis of importance and reliability, marked those places on a map where there were concentrations of Germans, noted the names of the factories that employed them and, in short, tried to find out everything he could use and could ask about without rousing surprise or suspicion.

Finally, he had a relatively clear picture. He already knew that the criminals had sought refuge in other countries of South America but now he was convinced that there was some reason why he had been sent here. He knew that here, in Argentina, these men tried to hide in small, out-of-the-way places and not in the capital where, among two hundred thousand Jews, there was always the danger of being recognized. They preferred to live in little groups, not far from one another, in unobtrusive suburbs of small cities, with a few medium-sized factories where they found work. Those who had enough money bought farms far from the city where they felt safe and were sometimes protected by a thick forest.

Adam Wahn didn't think for a minute that that was the sort of thing his man would do. Walz would want to live in the city. In a big city with nightlife, a lot of pretty women and gambling tables with big stakes; he'd want to be close to wine, horseracing, and adventure. Perhaps he was aware of the risk, but that was just part of the climate that actor needed to live. No doubt he also depended on a few influential friends and protectors. Men like him could do very well in this country. Since most influential people lived in the capital, Adam Wahn was sure not only that Walz was in this country but that there was also a fairly good chance he would find him in the hustle and bustle of this big, noisy city.

From the moment he began to believe he had been sent

on this road, from the day he was aware of what he really wanted to live for, he changed into a torch passed from hand to hand lighting his next step on the road to his goal.

At that moment, Adam Wahn began to believe in God. There were one or two details he might still attribute to coincidence but coincidences couldn't connect themselves into such an intentional chain. Some outside force was needed to organize things one after another, in their places, in a consistency that left no room for doubt. And the moment he began to believe, a quiet descended on him, a calm and peace he had never known. He was never again driven or fervent or compulsive about the deep wish for revenge that had brought him on this long journey. It wasn't he who was taking revenge but God Himself Who had decided that Esther's murderer would have to be punished, and he, Adam Wahn, was now nothing but an instrument in the hand of God. There was no more need to rush. When and how God would use one of his tools—and he believed that God had many tools like Adam Wahn and every one of them was destined for a different mission— that was God's own decision.

Sometime during that period Adam Wahn began going to synagogue. Not to the big one on Avenida de Libertad or any of the magnificent places but to a little prayer house near the port. At first he came only on Friday night, then twice a week; finally, he went to morning prayers every single day before he left for work and, when he could, came to afternoon and evening prayers as well. Everything he had abandoned and forgotten years and years before now slowly came back to him. Childhood memories of his parents' home, things he had never thought of since he left, words and lines of prayers his lips hadn't whispered for so long, so very long—even Yiddish suddenly came back to him. Sitting in the little synagogue near the port, he felt as if he belonged with all those men praying at his side.

He also learned a lot of useful information from his new friends there. After prayers, some of them always stayed in the next room full of thick tomes on all the walls. There they'd sit around a long oak table to read together, to listen to the interpretations of the old rabbi who stayed with them, or simply to talk about this and that.

Whatever he could read in the holy books was hardly enough to make Adam Wahn a pious man. For even in what he cared about, what he was looking for here, the forest of obscurity and contradiction was particularly dense and impenetrable. God of course spoke often of revenge but, in most cases, these were accounts between nations, not individuals. Even when He did speak clearly—as when He said "Whoso sheddeth man's blood, by man shall his blood be shed"—that still didn't answer the question of how a man could punish the criminal without himself crossing the clearest line of all, the unequivocal "Thou shalt not kill." Somewhere in the Talmud, he found that a "*talmid hacham* who does not avenge himself and retains anger like a serpent is no real *talmid hacham*." But another time he heard the old rabbi quote from the same Talmud that "he who forbears to retaliate will find forbearance from God for all his failings."

None of that helped him very much, but he didn't really need help. He was satisfied with the milestones on his path, and he now believed that God wouldn't have led him this far if He hadn't chosen him, Adam Wahn, as His instrument to carry out this mission. Wahn's newfound piety came from this belief, which was a neverending source of strength for him.

His new friends and acquaintances proved their usefulness to him in another way. They were familiar with the place and knew just who in fact turned the wheels in which factory and where the engineers, senior officials, customers, and supervisors came from. From the strands of their talk, Wahn wove a canvas on which the clear outlines of a picture began to take shape; he could glimpse the best prospects of finding those who had been driven by fear and conscience out of the Reich that didn't last a thousand years, as they had been promised, and where the banner with the swastika no longer waved. No doubt they found their refuge in German factories or those financed by Germans, and Wahn was soon armed with a detailed list of such factories employing more post-war German immigrants than others.

Even when his circle of friends expanded, there was nothing he liked better than to come back from time to time to the little white house with the little garden, to his friends the Duvals. He couldn't have said why, but he was most comfortable with them. Sometimes, as soon as he appeared at the gate, they would stop still for a moment in a bizarre, improvised pose, as if they were acting a pair of garden-dwarfs for him, the kind you see at the gates of the nouveaux riches. Wahn knew he could really laugh only with them.

Charles Duval, once called Charlemagne, truly was a great man. He was full of ideas, saw what others didn't, knew about everything going on around him, always found the word that hit the nail on the head and, even though he had stopped performing in the circus a long time ago, still viewed the world as a ring where everything had to happen fast, with perfect precision and a healthy dose of humor, and where the element of surprise was never lacking.

"I'll find that bastard for you," he surprised Wahn one day when they were alone. They were now such close friends that Wahn often returned to the issue that weighed on his heart; but he never went so far as to confess that he was interested only in finding Walz and avenging Esther's death. He couldn't understand how his little friend guessed it since he hadn't given the slightest hint of his intention.

Yet, Charles Duval repeated with absolute certainty: "I'll find him for you. You don't even have to tell me his name. If he's here, he changed it long ago anyway. I'll find him. You can count on me. Duval knows what has to be done." He tapped his high forehead with his little finger — Wahn recalled that poor Leo Riesenberg used to do the same — and didn't talk about it anymore.

Not until two or three days later, when they were alone again, did Charles suddenly say, quite casually: "All I needed to be a general was about two feet. Without that, I wasn't in the army, I didn't fight in the war, and I had to watch everything that happened from the distance. But, don't worry, there are some battles even I know how to fight."

Then he revealed his plan.

Mrs. Duval's family, the Avellanedas, was one of those ancient, aristocratic clans that base their success on the wisdom that says that a tree, even with a sturdy trunk, stands in all tempests only if its branches are spread out properly. According to this golden rule, before old Alberto Avellaneda was laid to rest in the family vault of hewn marble, he saw to it that each of his six sons had a different piece of the pie. The oldest inherited the family farm in La Pampa, the second went into industry (including a partnership in the factory where Wahn worked), the third was a high-ranking officer, the fourth was a priest, the fifth exported meat and hides, and the sixth and youngest, Fernando Avellaneda, went into politics with Peron and now had a high position in one of the trade unions. Except for the priest, Rosita's brothers also paved their way to new places with marital connections so that the family tree branched out splendidly and grew higher and broader.

"Fernando," Charles Duval now decided, tapping his brow again in praise of his own wisdom. Then he explained to Wahn what had occurred to him.

Like every great plan, this one too was very simple. Duval knew what Adam Wahn didn't—that Peron's government compelled all laborers to be organized and registered in trade unions. In the card catalogue of the federation offices, a photograph had to be attached to every member's card. Maybe even more than one photo because the index cards were arranged not only alphabetically but also according to factory. You could surely assume that almost all the post-war immigrants from Germany had found work in German industries, and Wahn already had the lists of these firms. Which companies belonged to German owners was hardly a secret among the management of the professional federations. So, there was nothing easier than to go over the photographs of the employees of these companies since, after all, there wasn't an infinite number of them. Though not an absolutely sure bet, it was quite likely that, if the man Wahn was looking for really was in Buenos Aires, his picture would show up.

So simple. Adam Wahn couldn't forgive himself for not

thinking of such an obvious possibility. When he had gone to work in the factory, he too had had to join a professional federation, fill out a mile-long questionnaire and attach some passport photos to it. While Wahn was cursing his own stupidity, Charles Duval was already at work. That very evening, he invited his brother-in-law Fernando, explained the issue to him and, without mentioning Wahn, found some reason why it was important for him to find out everything he could about a man who was hiding out under an assumed name but whom he would easily recognize from a picture. Two days later Fernando began bringing the employee cards of each German company in Buenos Aires, one after another. At night Wahn would go over them, and each day Fernando would exchange them for new ones. On the fifth day Wahn found what he was looking for.

The man in the photo on the card in Wahn's hand called himself Enrico Valdes. Evidently Heinrich Walz couldn't find anything closer to the old name that he had had to give up but didn't want to part with altogether. Even if he had chosen a different name, the face in the picture dissipated all doubts about his identity. Even if the moustache above the thick lips was thinner than the one engraved in Wahn's memory and the square face with almost no expression was now enclosed in a frame of mutton-chop whiskers, it was impossible to mistake the high cheekbones, the receding chin, and the eternally half-closed eyes that looked as though they were swimming in a pit of grease.

Wahn's hands, with the juggler's strong, precise, trained fingers, now trembled for the first time in his life. He had come to the end of his journey. Here was the man he had been seeking for so long. The card gave the name of the company where Heinrich Walz, alias Enrico Valdes, was employed and his place of residence. Wahn knew both the factory and the street where Walz lived. More than once he must have passed by his house without knowing how close he had been to his goal. Now he did. Now there was only the last step. How many times in these few months had he planned this step down to the last detail. Now, for the first time, he saw how difficult that step would be, how much he still had to check and prepare, and on how many rocks he was still liable to crash.

If Adam Wahn became a pious man, and if we can say exactly when and where it happened, it was probably on that evening when he held Walz's picture in his trembling hands, and the place was the little prayer house not far from the port where he used to go every day. On that day his mind wasn't on the words of the evening prayer. He prayed a different prayer that evening. Now he thanked God for bringing him here and giving him this chance to realize his goal. What he had only sensed before was now absolute certainty. He knew he hadn't reached that stage because he himself wanted to and it wasn't his will that would guide his hand at the decisive moment. More than that. The distinction between the one who gave the orders and the instrument that would carry them out suddenly began to blur. In that moment, Adam Wahn began to be one with his God.

He didn't know how he got back to his room from the synagogue that night. He didn't think he found the way home by himself. Someone must have brought him there, but he was too embarrassed to ask the landlady and she herself didn't mention anyone.

The next day he didn't go to work. He got up early, and by six o'clock in the morning he was standing opposite the building where Heinrich Walz, alias Enrico Valdes, lived.

Half an hour later, hidden behind a tree directly across from the entrance, he saw the man he was waiting for come out of the house.

In a raincoat he looked smaller than Wahn remembered. Adam Wahn's hand no longer trembled. With one well-aimed shot he could easily have fulfilled his mission even from where he was standing. The street in a quiet neighborhood, far from the big noisy city, was empty at that hour. But Walz's encounter with vengeance was not to be so easy.

The man in the raincoat got into a little red car parked in front of the house and drove away. Soon after the car moved off, so did Adam Wahn, who knew where to follow it. Now he walked like someone out for a morning stroll. He had no more reason to rush.

*20

In the parking lot in front of the factory there were more than two hundred cars, but from the distance Wahn saw only the one he was looking for. There were no guards, and it wasn't hard to determine that Walz hadn't bothered to lock his car. But even if he had, Adam Wahn wouldn't have had any trouble opening it. He was prepared for everything down to the last detail and had thought everything through to the very end.

Or almost to the very end. For he hadn't yet decided on one last thing: how he would strike the final blow. He had already decided against anything that might give Walz a quick death. For example, he could easily have planted a load of dynamite under the car, connected it to the starter, and watched from a safe distance as slivers of driver and car flew into the air. But Adam Wahn wasn't thinking of such things. Before he died, Walz would have to see his face, have to recognize who was taking revenge on him, identify him and know why he had to die.

But while he still didn't know how he was going to send Walz to the deepest part of hell, he was absolutely clear about what would happen before that final blow. He only had to find out what time the shift ended, and then he returned to his room in the widow Martinez's house, where he had lived since he had been led to Buenos Aires to fulfill the mission he would complete that day. Everything he needed was in the knapsack he had brought two years ago with all his earthly possessions. He had prepared everything long ago but checked once more to be sure nothing was missing. Then, since he still had lots of time, he decided to sleep a few hours. He took off his shoes and stretched out on the bed. But in spite of his firm decision, and even though he was absolutely certain of every one of his steps—except for the last—he was much too excited to fall asleep. So after a while he got up again, put on his shoes, and went out.

He walked wherever his feet took him and wasn't especially surprised when, at the end, he found himself in front of the white house of his little friends. Now, in March— which was already autumn there—no one was working in the garden. He opened the gate and went straight to the studio behind the house, where he was sure of finding Charles at that time of day. He wasn't wrong. Duval was sitting on a tall chair, his little legs dangling in the air, a canvas on an easel in front of him, a palette in one little hand and a brush in the other, working on a picture that would soon be finished. A still life with two fans, cards, a rose on a table, and, next to it, a pistol set with mother-of-pearl. But it was more than just a still life since the cards were in the hands of two players who seemed to be sitting opposite one another but couldn't be seen. The whole picture looked like a segment of a larger picture.

"I just wanted to tell you I've seen him," Wahn said after they had greeted one another. Duval just looked up from his work for a moment, nodded as a sign that he understood and went on painting.

"You planning to see him again?" he asked after a moment and paused again until Wahn answered.

"Yes. Today."

This time Duval didn't even look up. He just changed one of the cards from hearts to spades. Adam Wahn looked on for a little while as the picture grew and changed under the brush, following the quick, short movements of Duval's hand. Then he said goodbye.

He still had a lot of time. Once again he let his feet lead him and wound up at the little synagogue near the port. The prayer house was empty at that hour, with only a few old men sitting on the bench in the yard, as always, waiting for the next prayers. In the room next to the prayerhouse, whose shelves were crowded with books all along the walls, Wahn found the old rabbi reading a huge tome. He was shortsighted and read with his face so close to the book that it looked as if he and the book were one.

Wahn took a book off the shelf, sat down at the other end of the table, and opened it without trying to figure out the meaning of the words. He had time but he couldn't let himself be distracted from the one thing he had to do. He sat with his elbows on the table and closed his eyes behind the little awning he made of his fingers pressed to his brow. He didn't know how long he sat like that when, all of a sudden, he heard the rabbi's voice from the other end of the table.

"You're about to embark on a long journey, aren't you?"

"What? Journey?" he started, as if wakened out of a dream. "Who told you? How do you know that, rabbi?"

The old man smiled in reply and it seemed to Wahn as if his face framed in a white beard were suddenly lit up.

"Come, I'll give you a blessing," said the old rabbi after a moment, and Adam Wahn stood up, walked to the other end of the long table, and put his head under the lifted hands of the rabbi, which were already waiting for him. The old man put his hands on Wahn's forehead and his lips whispered the words of the blessing.

Then it was time for Wahn to be on his way. First he went home, put on a raincoat like the one he had seen Walz wearing that morning, and, taking the pack with all the things he needed, he walked back to the parking lot where Walz had left his car. He got there a long time before the workers came out of the factory. The car was still unlocked and he had no trouble getting into it since there was no one in the parking lot.

He didn't see Walz come out of the factory, but as soon as the car door opened he saw the man who dropped into the driver's seat without being seen himself. He waited on the floor behind the front seat for only a split second and, when Walz put the key in the ignition, Wahn grabbed him forcefully by the neck, pulled his head back, and stuffed his mouth and nose with a rag dipped in chloroform. A few seconds later the car moved out of the parking lot.

Wahn now sat behind the wheel, dressed in a raincoat

like Walz's, while Walz lay on the floor of the car. As more people were coming out to their cars, Wahn also put on the hat that had fallen off Walz's head. He drove on side streets where it wasn't likely that anyone would recognize the car. When they were outside the city, he stopped again, pulled Walz's hands around behind his back, and put handcuffs on them. He tied his feet with a rope. Nothing was lacking in his pack.

Now he drove along the bay. Many people were returning home from work at that hour, but when he left the last suburbs, traffic thinned out. After another twenty kilometers the road was practically empty, except for a few trucks passing now and then. He turned off the main road and went along an unpaved path to the shore. In summer these white beaches were full of people, but now, in March, the autumn rains had begun. Although it wasn't raining that day, the clouds were lowering over the sea and no one was likely to come here. Moreover, the waves were high and high tide was approaching.

Wahn didn't drive to where the car would sink in the sand but stopped near the rocks at the edge of the beach. He dragged the still unconscious and shackled Walz out of the car and sat him against a rock. Even if the man had been awake and had tried to call for help, his voice would have been swallowed up in the beating of the high billows of the stormy sea. No one and nothing could help him escape his punishment now.

Wahn took his pack out of the car, sat down a few feet from his prisoner, facing him, and waited for Walz to wake up. The dose of chloroform he had given Walz wouldn't last much longer. He took the pistol and the five colored billiard balls out of his pack and put them on the ground next to him. Then he stretched his arm to make sure it was steady, to see if his hands were trembling. Not a finger moved. He was calm. He just had to overcome his impatience. He had waited so long, he could wait a little while longer.

The first thing Walz saw when he came to was the man sitting opposite him on the sand, tossing colored billiard balls up in the air one after another, spinning them in a circle, catching them as they fell and throwing them up again, one after another, in an orbit. All of a sudden, he recognized the man sitting a few feet away from him. He tried to stand up and only then did he realize that his hands and feet were bound.

Veils dropped off his numbed senses. The man in front of him was tossing the billiard balls high up, and it seemed to Walz that they were moving in a circle coming closer and closer to him. Any minute, they might fall down on his head. Then he saw the pistol next to the juggler's leg. He began to whine like a trapped animal. First he called for help, then wailed wordlessly like a madman, but the only one who heard him was Adam Wahn, whose hands went on tossing the colored billiard balls in circles with the same unmoving persistence as then, years ago, in the court of Major Kohl. Except for him, there wasn't a living soul in the entire area, and the stormy sea drowned out even the pitiless laughter of the gulls whose wings, like arrows, penetrated the clouds hovering over the sea.

Each wave landed like the hand of a gambler putting his winning card on the table. No human voice could be heard beyond a few feet. At last Walz realized the futility of his shouts. When he grew quiet, Adam Wahn began to talk, all the while spinning the colored billiard balls in front of

Walz's terrified eyes. Not even the approaching darkness could shake the confidence of the juggler's movements.

"Shout. Roar till you lose your voice. Wail like a mad dog. No one will hear you," said Adam Wahn in a voice as even and calm as the circling billiard balls in front of Walz's face. "Remember? Recognize me?" Every word fell like the endless string of drops crashing incessantly on the skull of a medieval victim. "The Jewish scum. One of the thousands you knew, God knows how many you murdered. How could you know how many there were? Who counts the bugs he steps on, the insects he crushes? But just to be absolutely sure, I'll remind you of this one piece of scum who survived and will now squash you like a bug. Remember? A soirée at Major Kohl's. Even *your* memory can't be so bad. I'm sure you recognize the stinking Jew, one of Kohl's court jesters, the one whose wife you shot to death because you were furious that he didn't let you win a bet. Maybe you wouldn't have recognized me, but you couldn't forget these billiard balls spinning around in front of your eyes. You're seeing them today for the last time. This time, though, they won't stop moving on your command—but on mine. And that will be the sign that your end has come."

Walz's whole body trembled like a leaf. He no longer called for help. He began to beg for mercy and to whine like a beaten dog. Disjointed tatters of words came out of his mouth, contorted by fear, and Wahn didn't make any effort to understand them. He kept spinning the billiard balls, catching them just as they finished circling, just when he had to throw them up again in orbit. But he didn't take his eyes off Walz for a second. Walz looked straight ahead, terrified, following the balls in their orbit, then suddenly he knelt down and pounded his head on the ground until blood flowed from his brow. Finally, he began to crawl like a snake in the sand and to plead with Wahn with panicky and desperate eyes.

Suddenly he calmed down, crept back to the rock where Wahn had propped him up when he was unconscious, and stared mutely at the sea, endlessly thrusting its waves onto the shore. Wahn noted the dark stain spreading on Walz's trousers. Fear was making the superman wet his pants.

That was the moment Wahn decided to catch his colored billiard balls. He put them back in his pack and picked up the revolver that had lain next to his leg all the while.

Walz's whole body trembled again. Saliva dripped from his thick lips onto his quivering chin. Once again he began to whine and wail and weep and beg for mercy. Wahn was only sorry the man he had sought so long broke so quickly.

"You still have a little bit of time to be afraid," he said. "I haven't yet decided how I'm going to finish you off. Every death is too easy for a bastard like you. Should I just shoot you like a mad dog? That's too fast. Split your head with one of these billiard balls? You might not die immediately but you'd probably get knocked out and that's a blessing you don't deserve. Maybe I don't have to kill you at all. Maybe it would be better if I just shoot between your legs to castrate and cripple you forever. No, no. I promised myself that you wouldn't live out this day. Not even as a cripple. I'm only sorry I can't kill you more than once."

All his hatred and desire for revenge now overflowed into his words. It was hard for him to believe all the cruelty accumulated inside him. Even as he was saying all these dreadful words, he was beginning to doubt if he really could carry out all the things he heard himself saying. But he couldn't stop now. He had passed the point of no return. Walz had to die.

All of a sudden, he realized he wasn't talking to Walz like someone carrying out a sentence but was really arguing with himself about whether he was indeed an instrument in the hand of God as he had believed up to that moment. Walz, of course, couldn't have known about that internal dialogue since Wahn kept dripping hatred on him and his words fell on Walz's head like slow drops ripping up the last shreds of his mind.

"Or maybe," Walz now heard Wahn say, "I should put you back in that car, turn on the motor, and twist the exhaust pipe so the gas slowly fills up the air inside the closed windows. Remember? Just like you did. Or, maybe here's an even better idea: I'll take you in the car to where it begins to sink in the sand, throw the key far out into the ocean and leave the rest to God. Let Him decide whether the waves should carry you out to sea or wash you up on the shore."

All the while Wahn was thinking aloud, he was playing with the gun in his hand. All he had to do was aim it and pull the trigger and the mission he had prepared for all these years would be done. After all, he had been living only for that moment. So, why all this hesitation, these doubts, this uncertainty? Why was he delaying?

Never in his life had he killed anyone. His hands were still clean. If he killed Walz now, would he be any happier? Would he still be able to sleep? Walz obviously slept peacefully. If anything did disturb his sleep, it was fear and not bad conscience. But would he, Wahn, be able to close his own eyes? Could he measure himself by Walz's standard?

Did he want to compare with him in cruelty? Of course, God had brought him here. He was convinced of that. Here, on this beach, he now had to sit face to face with the murderer he had been seeking for years and years. Up to that moment, he was sure that God had chosen him to be His instrument, the rod of His wrath, to carry out the punishment and settle the account. Now he was wavering between two alternatives. What if this was only a test? What if God wanted to show him that he was no better than Walz, that he too could murder, that he too was a helpless human being? Doesn't punishment belong to God alone? And if it was His will to punish, did He need to choose a man as His instrument?

Adam Wahn was still playing with the gun in his hand, but he was beginning to believe less and less that he would really use it. If only the man in front of him would try to defend himself with a single word! But tearful pleas and the whining of a stricken animal were all that came out of his mouth, twisted in terror.

Suddenly that stopped too. Walz sat stricken with dread, fear and horror in his staring eyes. If I kill him now, thought Wahn, I'll have killed a helpless madman. Maybe a life in constant fear and lunacy is a worse punishment than death itself. But maybe what he read in Walz's panic-stricken eyes was nothing more than a fleeting fog. Maybe he would yet defend himself. To kill a man in battle with your own hands was another matter altogether.

He put down the gun and walked over to Walz. He untied the rope around his feet and took off the handcuffs. Then he waited. Walz didn't move. He remained seated, leaning on the rock, looking straight ahead as before.

"Get up," ordered Wahn and Walz scrambled up and stood at attention.

"I won't kill a helpless man. I'm not like you. Defend yourself like a man."

This time, Walz didn't carry out the order. Instead, he lifted his hands to his face, which was twisted even more by a new surge of fear.

"Coward! Rat!" Wahn cursed him to ignite his wounded masculine anger, but nothing helped. Perhaps he had to be humiliated even more to restore his fighting spirit. "Strip! Take off everything!" Wahn shouted orders, hoping that Walz would resist. But the man humbly took off his coat, trousers and shirt until he stood naked before Wahn just as Esther had stood before him that night.

Now, now, Adam Wahn said to himself. Now he should hurl himself on him and wring his throat until all his breath was gone. But the idea of touching that monster filled him with disgust. He felt nauseous. He had to breathe deeply so as not to vomit.

Then something strange happened to Walz. Suddenly he lifted both hands and, his eyes rolling madly, began to march to the sea. He came to the first wave and went on marching as if there was nothing there. He entered the wall of high waves that rose up in front of him and closed in behind him.

Now it was Adam Wahn who looked straight ahead at the sea, where darkness quickly fell and covered everything.

* *
21

He didn't know how long he stood there leaning against the rock. For a moment he seemed to merge into it. Later he remembered only that he threw every trace of himself into the pack, put it on his shoulder and took the shortest path to the main road where a truckdriver picked him up and brought him back to the city.

He also remembered that two things stayed in his mind on that trip. The first was that if something appeared in the newspapers in the next few days, it would only be a few lines about an abandoned car belonging to Heinrich Walz—no, to Enrico Valdes—being found on the beach near a pile of male clothing. It might be assumed that Valdes, who had been missing for three days, had drowned while swimming.

The police would not consider suicide for, in such cases, a person usually goes into the water fully clothed.

To his great surprise, it also occurred to him that, till that moment, he hadn't thought at all of the fact that his mission was finally completed. If he was capable of concentrating on anything, it was the feeling of infinite gratitude to God for taking the last step Himself, the only step Adam Wahn wasn't ready for despite all his years of preparation.

*   *   *

That was all he remembered, and that was all we heard from him. After this point in the story, we didn't see him anymore. The next day, when it was Max's turn to visit Wahn, they didn't let him in.

Wahn's condition suddenly took a turn for the worse, the high fever came back, and the doctors shrugged their shoulders. They either didn't know or didn't want to tell us what had caused the unexpected reversal. None of us, not even his friend from Mea Shearim, was allowed to see him. A week later he died. Then our awful suspicion was confirmed. After the amputation, the wound became infected and the spread of the poison couldn't be checked. Even now, no one could explain what caused the complication. My explanation—which I shared only with Max—was that Adam Wahn died after telling the story that had burdened his heart for so long. Now, if we could, we had to continue thinking about all those things. He had nothing more to add.

We buried Adam Wahn the day after he died. In the cemetery of Givat Shaul, along with Max and me, there was only the man of the key with no gate, who brought two others from Mea Shearim. Together with the four men of the burial society and the gravedigger, we made up a minyan. One of them said a prayer over the grave, the man whose house Adam Wahn had lived in those last years said Kaddish, each of us threw a shovel of dirt on the body wrapped in its prayer shawl, and the gravedigger finished his job and smoothed the soil.

The ants, the worms, and the beetles now started their job and the body of the juggler Adam Wahn began to crumble into dust and to join the dust of thousands of others in the great layer added to all the other layers piled on top of one another, lifting Jerusalem closer and closer to heaven.

Maybe, I said to myself, maybe I'm not far away either from the day when my dust will cling to the dust of others on rainy days and be one with the masses of earth and the stones of these mountains where a new Jerusalem will always emerge over the old. For all times, to all eternity.

22

We returned from the cemetery, walking slowly, our legs heavy and weary. Suddenly we were very old, and I, at least, had no desire to talk. Max too was silent. But his silence was the gentle yet menacing massing of clouds before a storm.

We walked for a long time without saying a word, until Max's clouds could no longer bear the weight of the accumulated questions. First he simply repeated over and over: "I don't know. I don't know. I don't know." I knew he was repeating his learned father's last words and the only answer his wise brother could give him when he kept asking why their beloved sister had to die so young.

"I don't know, don't know," he repeated several times

and the words sounded like the first heavy drops that herald a thunderstorm. Then he couldn't restrain himself any longer; he had to say it.

"There was a time," he began, "when I revolted. I rebelled against God and compared Him with the juggler Wahn who cared about only one thing. He wanted to survive and nothing in the world could divert him from the path to this single goal. Even the murder of his wife in front of his own eyes didn't take his mind off his goal. If it was so necessary to survive, even something like that couldn't stop his colored billiard balls, they had to spin in their orbit. Just as the planets in the universe kept in motion by another, greater juggler, don't stand still because millions of innocent children are murdered on this planet. Now I don't revolt anymore, now I know that it won't get me any closer to an answer, and I don't know whom to ask for forgiveness, God or Adam Wahn. As for Wahn, at least I know what made him act the way he did. First the desire to survive and then the desire to avenge. As for God? Why does He do what He does? Marta, Hilde, poor little Leo Riesenberg, Wahn's wife, and now Wahn himself. Why? I ask you, why?"

He didn't expect an answer. He knew the only answer I had was a shrug. But as the rain can't stop until the clouds are empty or until the wind scatters them, so Max couldn't stop asking:

"I know that the stars spin, and I can follow the movement of God's invisible finger in the sky. I even know something about the laws in force up there. But what about the laws down here? What is the meaning of the things He does here on earth?" He kept on with his long monologue of questions all the way back from the cemetery.

"As far as I know," he said abruptly, "maybe right at this

very minute, Adam Wahn is standing face to face with Him. I ask myself what I would say to Him if I were standing there. Years ago, there were thousands of questions I would have asked, but today there aren't any. I can live very happily without knowing how and why a seed sprouts or what ripens the fruit of the womb. I don't have to ask who tells the blind pup it's time to seek his mother's milk. I don't even ask why He created all the nations and destroyed some of them or what happens with all our thoughts and feelings after we die and they bury us as we buried Adam Wahn. I can live without knowing all that. But what I do want to know is if we're really like those little puppets you wind up and they jump up and down, run here and there, go in circles until the spring stops. And if that's how it is, I don't care how long my spring is. I just want to ask one thing. I'd say to him: 'God, tell me only one thing. Tell me, clearly just once what's good and what's bad and why what we think is good is often lost in suffering and misery while what we think is evil survives everything, is rewarded with fame and wealth and success.' That's the only thing I'd ask, but I already know I'll never get an answer."

After a while, he added, "Just as I know I'll never stop asking."

Then he was silent again, and so we went on our way slowly from the cemetery. I knew he'd come back to the subject often, but at that moment, I didn't expect any more questions so I was surprised, even shocked, when he suddenly asked:

"Has it ever occurred to you that He keeps us just like Major Kohl, just to amuse Himself? Maybe we're nothing but His court jesters."

That was like a blow to the head, and it took me some

time to recover. I tried to resolve the issue with light words.

"Even if that's so," I said, "you must admit that He lets us perform on the loveliest stage. Look at all this beauty around us."

Ignoring the light tone of my answer, Max went on. "Yes, stage, performance, theater, maybe even a puppet theater. Maybe the director pulls our strings as he likes and throws us out with the rest of the rubbish when he gets fed up with the show."

Once again, I had only one answer. "Say what you will. As a stage-setter, He has no equal."

I knew this wouldn't distract him so I wasn't surprised that he went back to his questions that night when, as always, we met again at Menachem's kiosk. The juggler's death evidently stirred up a whole swarm of questions in his brain. They chased one another through his head, and he brought them out for me one by one. But the burden was too heavy and I couldn't carry it any further.

"Do you think he died happy?" Max wanted to know. "He only wanted one thing, to take revenge. And he did take revenge even if it wasn't exactly the way he planned. But are you sure it brought him peace? Did he really find what he was looking for?"

What else could I do but shrug? But the wise Menachem Salz (I really must tell you much more about him some day), even though he didn't know Adam Wahn and knew about him only what he had heard from us, had a ready-made answer as always.

"You know, it's like that. A man often finds something other than what he's looking for. You go to the forest to look for mushrooms and come back with a bucket of black-berries. The important thing is not to stop looking. Even if you don't always find exactly what you're looking for, you always find something you can use."

"Wahn sought revenge and found God," I grasped the string of Menachem's remarks, but Max tore it up with more questions.

"Found, found, you say? Maybe he found God, but did he also understand Him? Imagine you're getting lost, wandering around endlessly in the forest and, just when you're exhausted and almost fainting, you finally come upon somebody whom you can ask the way. That is, you can ask on condition that the two of you understand one another. But if you don't have a common language, even if you ask a hundred times, you won't get an answer. So what good is such a meeting?"

Again it was Menachem who had a reply.

"No, that's not how it is," he said, without having to think very much. "The one you meet can help you even if you don't speak the same tongue. Maybe he just smiles at you or stretches out his hand to you or gives you a friendly pat on the back. That encourages you and makes the rest of the journey easier. But there's also another possibility. The man you meet is also going somewhere. If you can't find your own way, why not go with him? Wherever you end up, at least it's better than groping in the dark all by yourself."

"That's probably what Wahn did," I said, trying to draw as much as possible out of Menachem's wisdom. "Or at least that's what I understood. His search was hopeless until he understood that he had to leave the decision in God's hands, and then he just went wherever he believed God led him. He reached his goal and was finally glad that God finished the job in His own way."

"Do you have some other name for that notion besides bankruptcy?" asked Max aggressively as he rummaged angrily in his thin beard with his bony fingers.

"A man can reconcile himself to something without being bankrupt," I objected, even though I knew I didn't sound either convinced or convincing. Even Menachem didn't try to help us out now. Max was silent, however, and though I wasn't sure he had grasped my objection, when he shook himself and began talking again, I had the impression he had taken another tack.

"As I stood at Adam Wahn's grave today," he said, "I asked myself: When did he really die? Didn't the bullet that killed his wife put an end to his life too? Was it Adam Wahn who didn't strangle the murderer on the spot but went on throwing and catching his billiard balls? Or was that somebody else? Or maybe he died years later, on the abandoned beach where, after a long search, he had taken the man on whom he had to take revenge. Then he learned that, despite the hatred that had accumulated inside him day and night for years, he was not capable of killing. Didn't Adam Wahn die then? Or was it a while later, when he saw Walz leave life so differently from what he had been planning for years? Or maybe he really died yesterday?

"I also asked myself," he went on, "if he really did die only now—even though it's hard for me to believe that—what kept him alive till now and what finished him off now? To him, everything was an expression of God's will. The fact that he didn't have to kill Walz and that Walz killed himself was God's will. Just like the fact that he found Walz, who was hiding on the other side of the world, like finding a needle in a haystack, that was also the finger of God. Everything that happens in the world is God's will. That's what he believed. Nothing could happen against that will, and anyone who resisted would perish. And there's no place in the world where a man's closer to the will of God than in Jerusalem. Wahn believed that, so he came here to die one more time."

"And that's what you call bankruptcy?" I tried to bring him back to the idea he expressed earlier.

"Yes, bankruptcy," he replied without thinking much. "If everything in the world is the finger of God, then the death of Wahn's wife must also be. And the fact that Wahn—God knows when was the last time he left Mea Shearim—would be in Machane Yehuda market exactly when the bomb went off that wounded and finally killed him—that's also the finger of God. By the way, I couldn't help asking our friend from Mea Shearim what had brought Wahn to Machane Yehuda that day. He hemmed and hawed for a bit but in the end came out with the truth. His older brother, a rabbi in Buenos Aires, had sent Wahn to him. Now this brother wrote asking him to deliver a message to a man on Agrippas Street near the market. He himself had to be in the Old City that day to supervise the building of the synagogue so he asked Wahn to take it for him. That was also the finger of God. Strange are His ways and we must learn to understand them. And nowhere can you hope to learn them better than in Jerusalem. Study from morning to night, try to understand the meaning of things. But you can't change them because everything is the finger of God. That's pretty much how Adam Wahn must have seen things. And that's what I call bankruptcy."

"What about you?" I asked him straight out.

"I told you. We're all bankrupt in our own way. I avoid bankruptcy by declaring my willingness to give in. I accept the fact that I'll never know. I've reconciled myself to it. It doesn't change much, but at least I don't give myself any illusions."

It grew late. The street leading to Jaffa Gate had been quiet for some time. Only the three of us still stood there and Menachem had already put all the perishables in the icebox. As he stacked up cases of bottles and straightened up the kiosk, he spoke as if he were weighing each word.

"I'm not an educated man, like you are. And my grandfather Ephraim, who held my hand when I walked with him and taught me all he knew, was also a simple man. He taught me that there will always be more things we'll never know than things we can learn. But he used to tell me that it's more important to know when your neighbor needs help than to understand everything the Holy-One-Blessed-Be-He intends. Maybe He's busy and doesn't have time to think about old widow Pinkus around the corner or maybe for a moment He forgot poor crippled Levy. So you come in meanwhile and help out as much as you can. God won't hold it against you. That's how my grandfather Ephraim saw things, and I think he was right."

Suddenly we didn't talk about Adam Wahn anymore and, more importantly, not about revenge either but about help. That's how it always is with Menachem. Some day I really must tell you a lot more about him.

23

Menachem's simple wisdom always worked like a night-cap; you could feel the sweet warmth spreading, flowing into your veins, turning into a blessed calm that made your eyelids heavy. But this time Menachem's words didn't have the usual effect. Of all the things that went through Max Himmelfarb's mind, at least one thought he had expressed aloud remained deeply etched in my brain. What if all of us were only court jesters, kept to amuse the Almighty Lord of our life and death?

I couldn't get away from it. I floundered around in the question like a fish caught fast in a net. I didn't get much sleep that night, and when I did fall asleep for a moment, I found myself in my dream back in the court of Major Kohl.

Thousands were dying terrible deaths all around us and only we four court jesters were still alive—we always survived. Dressed in striped tatters that hung on us as on scarecrows, we ran around and around the long table in the big room where Major Kohl entertained his guests at soirées. I came first, waving my arms and imitating a bird but with the hump on my back and my big head deep between my shoulders, I looked more like a bat. Then came the stargazer, Max Himmelfarb, advancing with the hops and jumps of his long legs, all the while putting his eye to the cardboard tube as if he were observing the stars with a telescope. After him was the dwarf with the funny name of Leo Riesenberg, rolling his hoop and twisting himself around through people's legs. At the end of the procession, the juggler Adam Wahn tossed colored billiard balls up in the air and spun them around in their orbit.

Then suddenly we were no longer running around the long table with Kohl's two big dogs underneath, the German Shepherd named Wolf and the Great Dane named Brutus. Instead we were running quickly down the street leading to Jaffa Gate and through all the streets of Jerusalem. We must have changed the order of our procession, for the dwarf and the juggler were now in front of us and Wahn tossed the billiard balls into the air with only one hand. The dwarf didn't roll skulls but caught the billiard balls just when he had to throw them up again and put them in Adam Wahn's one hand which still had five agile fingers that could spin five, six, seven billiard balls high in their orbit. Leo was fast and nimble and they seemed to be coordinated nicely but, every time, in spite of all their agility, one ball would leave the circle and roll into a pit gaping in our path, like an open grave. Then I always woke up.

THE COURT JESTERS
176

After this dream had recurred God knows how many times, I decided to get up. It must have been close to dawn. I hadn't slept much, and when I did doze off for a moment, the dreams spinning in front of my eyes, like the juggler's colored billiard balls, hadn't left me alone. Nevertheless, I didn't feel tired. I got dressed and took a walk toward Jaffa Gate, along the walls of the Old City, to a certain rock where I come to sit from time to time and do some thinking. I usually come alone but I had also been there with Max and once or twice with Menachem Salz. Sometimes I come during the day and sometimes at dusk but I had never been there so early in the morning.

The stars were still stuck to the sky, but they were already turning pale and seemed to be fading. Years and years ago I had watched deer leaving a meadow and melting into the forest. Now, watching the stars that seemed to be going away, I remembered that view from long ago. For a while I held my breath just like then.

There wasn't a living soul anywhere around. Bats were still hanging from the rafters of the caves and from the beams of the bell towers where they had returned after their nocturnal hunting; weasels and field mice came back to their holes and burrows; the birds were still sleeping on the boughs of the olive trees and in the tops of the pines and cypresses; and the lizards hadn't yet crawled out from under the stones—they too seemed sleepy at this hour of the morning.

If He existed and if He wanted to tell me something, this was the moment. We were all alone. Just He and I. He could have talked only to me and no one would have heard and no one would have known. If He had wanted to uproot the tree of my doubt—and its roots had grown deeper and broader in me ever since Max Himmelfarb said what hadn't occurred to me—now was the time.

"What if He does keep all of us just to amuse Him? Like clowns, like court jesters? Just like the mighty Major Kohl?" That's what Max had asked, and though I refused to accept it, I didn't know how to get rid of it, how to stop what suddenly threatened to fall down on me and bury me under its weight. Are there perhaps more possibilities of fleeing from here, from this life, than from the hell ruled by Major Kohl? And if He existed at all, didn't He rule over our life and death even more than Kohl? My doubts quickly grew higher and wider, and if He wanted to get them out of my mind, there was no better moment than now.

Then, just when the gloom that had clung to me ever since Max expressed his thought reached the point of deepest darkness—just then it happened.

At first, only a thin strip of light appeared, as if someone had shot an arrow the color of bare young branches, an arrow that flew all along the broad bow stretching over the horizon and hovered lightly. And as through the crack of a slowly opening shell, mother-of-pearl appeared and slowly trickled down onto the slopes of the distant mountains and climbed up into the skies above them. For a moment, it looked like a row of gleaming teeth between the soft lips of a beautiful woman waking from a calm sleep with a caressing smile and taking off veils of purple mist. But the city and the land that stretched out before me all the way to the mountains of Moab were already beginning to change, this time into a sea of gardens of apricot blossoms. Only then did the pink melt into ochre and the stones and the walls and the mountains and the thin cypresses and the ancient olive trees each take on form as if they had been kneaded by the fingers of time using rain and wind and sun like the artisans in the street leading to Jaffa Gate use hammers and blowtorches and saws.

Somewhere, in one of the clay huts on the slopes of the City of David, the first rooster crowed his greeting to the newborn day. Meanwhile the light began to march, and before I woke up from the magic and recovered from the beauty I had been allowed to see, it reached not only the place where I was sitting on the rock but went through to the last crack and crevice and came into my eyes and through them to every blood cell that flows in my veins.

Only now did I suddenly know that the blood cells in me were also spinning in a fixed orbit, like the orbits of the heavens where every one of the millions of stars moves in the universe. That meant that every blood cell was just as important as the planets and the stars I saw before in the sky, now flooded before my eyes with the brightness of a blue and gold day. And not only the stars and not only me but every one of the thousands of birds in the treetops who now began to sing and every anemone and every cyclamen blooming on the slope in front of me, every butterfly and every stone and every clod of ground and every blade of grass, everything, even the hump on my back, everything had its place and its reason, its task and its fixed goal.

I knew I would never know—even if I never stopped asking—what was behind all that, why the stars spin in the universe and the blood cells in my veins; but one thing was clear to me at that moment: So much unimaginable beauty couldn't have been created without a purpose. And those who were allowed to stand and wonder at all this beauty couldn't have been created only to amuse their Creator. They weren't meant to serve Him as court jesters. More than that I didn't know. But that at least I knew.

It was a lovely day, the kind of day found here in this city more often than anywhere else in the world. If I were an artist, I would paint such days in copper and honey with the banner of the blue sky waving overhead. It seemed that an eternity must have gone by since my sleepless night— interrupted a hundred times by my recurrent nightmare about the juggler with one arm, the dwarf who would never unite the Lilliputians of the world, the stargazer with no stars, and the judge refusing to pass judgment—had gotten me out of my bed. In fact, it was no more than a couple of hours. I knew that because, as I walked back slowly, I saw the city waking up to a new day like everything else around me.

Like every morning, the street leading to Jaffa Gate began to echo with the ring of hammers, the roar of motors, and the high-pitched hum of saws. As I approached the kiosk on the corner, Menachem Salz was crossing the street as on every morning at this hour, carrying a copper tray loaded with steaming cups of coffee to the porters sitting on the steps in the doorway of the moving company, waiting for the day's work. After breakfast each of them will put a load on his shoulders and take it where it's supposed to go.

I really must tell you more about the porters in my street. Someday I will. I promise.